LOVING THE RAIN

JEFF LaFERNEY

Jeff LaFerney

TOWER
PUBLICATIONS

Jeff La Ferney

LOVING THE RAIN

Published by
Tower Publications

Dedication

I'd like to dedicate the publishing of this book to my past, present, and future students at Davison Community Schools. I've had and will continue to have such a rewarding experience working with kids, but I came to the realization that while challenging you, maybe I also had something more to offer. I began to consider stretching myself, wondering if maybe I was not living up to my own potential. I don't know if completing this project will inspire you, but I'm certain that you have inspired me. I hope many of you will read this novel, and it will influence you to reach your own goals.

Jeff La Ferney

Acknowledgements

I would like to give thanks to God who gave me the tools, the ideas, and the abilities to write this first book of mine. I would like to give special thanks to my wife, Jennifer, who has been patient and supportive throughout this project, and who helped me with my initial editing and gave me an idea that I ran with. I love you. Thanks go to my kids, Torey and Teryn, who simply are awesome kids; I'm very fortunate to be blessed by the two of you. I thank my parents, as well, who read my manuscript, and as always, encouraged and supported me in this project. I'm grateful for your guidance and constant love. I get most of my confidence from the two of you. Thanks also go out to Dallas, Andrea, Trish, and Susan, who all willingly volunteered to read my novel when the first draft was complete and gave support, encouragement, advice, and/or revision suggestions to me. Finally, thanks, Thad, for your medical insights. I am grateful for my friends.

Jeff La Ferney

Prologue

(October, 1986) When the National Anthem concluded, the fans clapped politely and then focused their attention on the two football teams that gathered on their opposite sidelines. The red, orange, and yellow leaves of the trees surrounding the football field were occasionally fluttering to the ground, propelled by a cool, autumn breeze. It was a Friday in mid-October and Okemos High School and Haslett High School were playing a non-league football game. Jack Harding leaped into the air, a single index finger extended skyward as he ran out with the kick coverage team for the Okemos Chiefs, a high school just east of Lansing, Michigan. He placed the kicking tee on the forty-yard line and prepared to boot the opening kickoff. Clay Thomas puffed his cheeks and blew a stream of white vapor between his facemask bars as he trotted out with the return team for the Haslett Vikings, a high school about five and a half miles away. There was a great crowd turnout for the neighboring schools, and there was excitement in the air.

Clay was a widely known pre-season all-state linebacker as well as a terrifying blocker and runner from his fullback position. Jack happened to be a very good soccer player who was convinced to perform double duty as the kicker for his high school team, but a first-year kicker's reputation doesn't go as far as a three-year star linebacker's, so, though Jack knew of Clay, Clay did not know of Jack. An excited cheer rose from the crowd as Jack approached the tee and booted a long kickoff. The Haslett kick returner received the football on the six yard line and headed up field behind his blockers. He wound his way toward the mid-field sideline, following Clay. An excited cheer began to rise from the Haslett cheering section as Jack Harding quickly became the last remaining obstacle standing in the way of a long kickoff return. Clay Thomas focused in on Jack and made a crushing block that literally sent him airborne to land on his back near mid-field. Haslett's returner sprinted the remaining fifty yards, escorted by Clay, and scored a touchdown on the opening kick. Jack Harding lay curled on his side for a good five minutes, trying with great difficulty to breathe.

There had been an explosion of fan noise as Jack was pummeled, followed immediately by laughter from many of the lesser mature Haslett fans. Jack had managed to roll over to witness the celebration of Clay's teammates, and a few minutes later had to endure the embarrassing sympathy cheer of the crowd as he was helped off the field. The pain, sounds, and images became permanently burned into Jack Harding's mind. But that early game experience was nothing in comparison to what happened at the end of the game. The score was tied with just four seconds on the clock and the ball on Haslett's seven yard line. It would be just a 24 yard field goal to win the game, and Jack hadn't missed a field goal of *any* length throughout six season contests. Haslett's coach called for a time-out before the snap to freeze the kicker, so both teams headed off the field to their opposite benches.

Jack Harding walked over to Clay. In the cocky way that he had perfected, Jack said, "Looks like you're gonna lose, Thomas."

Clay Thomas was not an ordinary high school teenager. He had discovered the ability to manipulate minds and literally make people do what he wanted. But Clay didn't ordinarily use his powers to influence the minds and behavior of other people. He had an inherent sense that keeping his powers and his secret to himself was a very wise course of action. Jack Harding, however, had just given him good motivation to alter those values, so he looked Jack in the eyes and said very calmly, "You will never make this field goal. You can't make it." Then off the field he jogged.

As the teams lined up for the last play of the game, Okemos's kicker was sweating. Something in his head kept saying, "*You can't make it.*" He made eye contact with Clay Thomas at his outside linebacker's position, and he heard in his head once again, "*You will never make it.*" As the perfect snap arrived in the holder's hands and a perfect hold was placed on the ground, Jack Harding stepped and swung his kicking foot. In his nervousness and uncertainty, he almost missed the football. It squirted off the toe of his cleat at about a 25 degree angle to the right. Opportunistically, Clay Thomas managed to scoop up the ball and started running for the opposite end zone. Only one player had any chance of tackling Clay—Jack Harding. Clay reached out and gave Jack a stiff-arm that sent him tumbling head over heels, his right-footed kicking cleat flying up in the air. With no time remaining, Clay ran the ball all the way for a touchdown and a six-point win. Jack Harding was humiliated, and it was a humiliation that he would never be able to shake.

***

(January, 1987) Lansing area weather reports were predicting a heavy snowfall, but a large crowd was nonetheless in attendance as Clay Thomas's Haslett Vikings and Jack Harding's Okemos Chiefs returned to the court after a time-out near the end of the second quarter. As his team prepared for the non-league basketball game, Jack's coach had discussed a game plan that mentioned Clay Thomas, who was the third leading scorer in his conference. Jack's name was never mentioned in Clay's practice preparation for Okemos. Three cheerleaders completed round offs and several back handsprings before scampering off the court. There was just 1:12 left in the second quarter of a very close game when Jack attempted a pass to a teammate. The home Haslett crowd erupted as Clay stole the pass and headed to the opposite end for a layup. Jack, who was still ticked off about the duel humiliations at the hands of Clay three months earlier, sprinted back and angrily shoved him in the hip as he released his shot. The referee immediately blew his whistle as the shot banked off the glass and teetered on the rim before falling through the net. Jack was called for a flagrant foul, giving Clay two free throws and the ball out of bounds.

With time running down in the fourth quarter, however, Jack's Okemos Chiefs still managed to be ahead by three points. When a Viking teammate drove to the basket and missed a layup, Clay jumped for the offensive rebound. He cradled the ball in his right hand and threw down a thunderous dunk. The ball flew through the rim and net and bounded off Jack Harding's forehead. Clay hung on the rim for a brief second and then dropped to the floor, landing face-to-face with Jack, who aggressively shoved his opponent in the chest. A referee quickly stepped between the two boys, then blew his whistle and signaled a technical foul.

The referee reported the foul to the official scorer and then cleared the end of the court for Clay's free throws. There was only three seconds remaining in the game. Jack's coach angrily yelled, "You *idiot*! You couldn't possibly have made a more boneheaded play, Jack! What were you thinking? That temper of yours might've just cost us the game!"

"He's a jerk, Coach. He deserved it."

Clay proceeded to make both free throws, putting Haslett ahead by a single point. The coach's screaming and berating continued without pause until the ball was set to be inbounded. He then grabbed a handful of jersey and literally hurled a substitute toward the scorer's table in an attempt to replace Jack.

The horn sounded at the scorer's table, but the referee jogged over to the bench. "It's too late to send your substitute into the game, Coach. He didn't report in on time."

The coach was fuming, but Jack had to stay in the game. He composed himself enough to match up defensively with his man. Haslett's inbounds passer was unable to find an open man and panicked. His poor pass was deflected by an Okemos player and incredibly ended up in Jack's hands with only two seconds remaining on the clock, and a Haslett defender foolishly reached in and was called for a foul that would send Jack to the free throw

10

line for a redeeming chance to win the game. Jack Harding then made another colossal mental blunder. He walked up to Clay and said, "Guess we're gonna win anyway."

Clay responded without much thought. It never even occurred to him that this was the same moronic kicker that boasted during the football game. Because Clay's conscience didn't bother him so much when he was dealing with idiots, he made careful eye contact with the fool from Haslett and very calmly said, "You *know* that you will *not* make your free throws."

Jack tried to shake off the amazing doubt he immediately felt, so he said, "I'll make 'em."

Clay didn't even speak. Just using his mind, his thoughts communicated, "*You will NEVER make them.*"

Jack stepped to the free throw line for a one-and-one and nervously prepared to shoot. "*I'm gonna miss,*" he thought. He took a deep breath, tried his best to relax, and then proceeded to leave the shot at least eight inches short of the rim, a ridiculous air ball. But the game wasn't over because the referee called a lane violation on the Vikings, three players having stepped into the free throw lane, not expecting the ball to miss the rim completely, and Jack got a second chance. Chants of "Air ball! Air ball!" came from Haslett's student section as teenagers wrapped fingers around their necks and made gagging and choking gestures. As Jack nervously prepared for another try, he could not shake the unmistakable belief that he had no hope of making the free throw. Before the attempt, Jack told himself, "*Don't be short again.*" He bounced the ball several times, took another deep breath, and launched his second free throw. The shot was so long and left, that it bounced off the backboard before bounding high into the air off the left side of the rim. A teammate of Jack's tipped it back up in the air, starting the game clock, and when the ball came down, Clay jumped high, grabbed it with his elbows out and landed, as the horn sounded, with an elbow squarely on the bridge of Jack Harding's nose, breaking the bone instantly. Clay celebrated with his team, never having even known he hit Jack. Meanwhile, Jack stalked off the floor, his nose bleeding, while both teams shook

11

hands. Clay never gave Jack another thought. As he exited the floor, Jack couldn't help but hear the laughter and jeers and see the scorn of his teammates.

Harding was forced to miss three games because of the injury and was pulled from the starting lineup for the remainder of the season, two facts that he blamed on Clay and for which he never forgave him. The two encounters that Clay Thomas had with Jack Harding completely escaped Clay's memory, but Jack would never forget.

***

(January 1992) Jessie Thomas drove herself to the hospital emergency wing and pulled right behind a paramedic's ambulance before stumbling out of her car. Two paramedics saw the pregnant woman as she temporarily lost consciousness on the pavement just steps from her car door. They rushed immediately to the fallen woman. Jessie awakened and appeared confused. She was breathing rapidly as a paramedic checked her pulse. When he felt her cool, clammy skin and noticed her pale skin color, he said, "Looks like hypovolemic shock. We need to get her inside *now*!" The emergency technicians placed Jessie on a gurney and quickly rolled her through the emergency room doors. The paramedic called out, "Tech to the front!" The triage nurse appeared immediately. "Call in stat for L and D!"

As she was rushed to the elevator in route to Labor and Delivery, the other paramedic said, "I need to ask a couple of questions, okay? Could you tell me your name and age?"

"It's Jessie. Jessie Thomas," she managed to reply. "I'm 21."

"How many weeks pregnant are you?"

"Just 30…I'm not due for almost two months," she barely managed to answer.

The paramedic instructed the triage nurse. "Call up. We have a 21-year-old female, 30 weeks pregnant. She appears to be in hypovolemic shock."

"You need to call, Clay. Please, call my husband…something's wrong! I think I'm having the baby!" Jessie weakly cried out.

12

***

In Labor and Delivery, they removed maternity clothing and were preparing an ultrasound when the nurse exclaimed, "I see a foot. The baby's breech!" She instructed another nurse, "Notify Dr. Nordstrum in O.R. We have a breech birth!" With no hesitation, Jessie was rushed to the operating room.

***

While the check-in nurse in the emergency room was dialing for Clay Thomas, he unexpectedly appeared at the window. "My wife, Jessie Thomas, was just rushed in. What's wrong?"

Clay was immediately directed to Labor and Delivery, who then directed him to the O.R. waiting room.

While filling out paperwork, he waited impatiently for nearly an hour for news about his wife and baby. Finally Dr. Nordstrum appeared and spoke with Clay. "Mr. Thomas, I'm Dr. Nordstrum."

Clay jumped to his feet. "Are my wife and baby okay?"

"We had to perform an emergency C-section on your wife. It was a difficult delivery, and there were complications, but both your wife and your son are okay for now."

"My son? We had a boy?" Clay was obviously proud, but then the words "for now" sunk in. "What do you mean?"

"Please, sit down, Mr. Thomas." Clay and the doctor both took seats. "The baby was breech. That *is* more likely for pre-term babies like yours. I assume you and your wife knew the baby was breech?"

"Yes, but we expected it to turn eventually. She wasn't due for almost two months."

"Well, her water broke, and unfortunately she went into labor. She was admitted in hypovolemic shock. While in Labor and Delivery, a foot emerged, but it was clear that her cervix had not dilated enough for the baby's head to make it, so she was rushed to the O.R. and we performed the emergency Cesarean section. When we removed the little guy, you may be interested in hearing, his right arm was extended alongside his head in perfect shooting position, just like a jump shot," the doctor smiled.

Clay couldn't resist smiling himself. Then he frowned. "There were complications."

"Two complications actually," the doctor replied. "In about 15 to 18 percent of footling breeches, the child is born with a prolapsed umbilical cord. The cord was wrapped around the baby's throat when we removed him. We had to revive the child. Oxygen deprivation had clearly occurred from cord prolapse, and if oxygen deprivation is prolonged—and there's no way of telling how long he was oxygen deprived—it may cause permanent neurological damage. Only time will tell with your son." There was a pause. "The other complication is with your wife. In this kind of emergency birth, there's always risk of injury to the mother's internal organs. In Jessie's case, the integrity of the myometrial wall was breached. Her uterus was ruptured. We had to perform an emergency hysterectomy. We didn't remove her ovaries, but your wife won't be able to have other children."

***

In time, Clay was able to see Jessie in the recovery room. The moment she saw Clay, she started weeping. "Is our baby gonna be all right?"

"The doctor said only time'll tell, but he's beautiful, Jessie. He's so little, but he's perfect. Did the doctor tell you," Clay asked in an attempt to cheer up his wife, "he was delivered in perfect shooting form? He's gonna be a ballplayer, you wait and see."

She cried louder instead. "I wanted lots of kids, Clay, and so did you. I'm so sorry."

Clay was a high school baseball coach, so the idea of not being able to provide a team full of kids for her husband to coach had left Jessie distraught. She was more than upset, she was anguished, and even though Clay himself was deeply hurting from the events he had just witnessed, he couldn't bear to see the woman he loved in such misery. When she continued to blame and torture herself, Clay had finally had enough. The things he had seen had saddened him in a way from which he wasn't sure he could recover, but he simply couldn't let the woman he loved continue to torment herself. Clay knew he had the power to change things, and though he would have to break a promise that he had made to himself when he met Jessie, he was compelled to manipulate her mind.

As she cried, Jessie caught her hurting husband's moist brown eyes, and he began to control her mind. "I want you to forget what happened this afternoon," Clay calmly said. "As soon as you knew something was wrong, we rushed to the hospital. You are not to blame. You gave birth to a beautiful baby boy, and you will love him with all your heart." Jessie was staring intently into Clay's eyes. "Jessie, forget this afternoon. You did nothing wrong. Do not ever believe in any way that you are at fault. Our only child is perfect."

"Our only child is beautiful and perfect."

"Yes," Clay said.

"There's no need for me to blame myself. It wasn't my fault."

"That's right, Jessie. I love you."

"I love you too, Clay."

Jeff La Ferney

Chapter 1

Standing outside the grocery store with his 17-year-old son, Tanner, 40-year-old Clay Thomas was watching the pouring rain. He hated it when it rained. He always had, as far back as he could remember. It had poured at his mother's funeral. He recalled standing at the gravesite, twelve years old, feet soaked from the splatter as he stood under an open black umbrella, staring at his mother's grave while it filled with water. He recalled stories about how he and his mother had both almost died during his childbirth, a delivery in an ambulance on the way to the hospital. Ironically, ten years later, Clay's mother had again almost died while attempting to save Clay from drowning in a lake. Lightning was flashing in the distance, so Clay's mother called for her son to leave the floating dock and return to the shore. He wasn't a particularly good swimmer, so when he began tiring, he panicked and started flailing in the water. His mother was carefully watching, so she dove in to help him. Neither mother nor son was doing well when Mr. Thomas rescued them with two floatation cushions from the pontoon boat that he was returning to the dock. Once the family was all safely on the dock, the rainstorm descended and Clay's mother started laughing from relief. The near drowning, and somehow the thunderstorm, had made a greater impression on his memory than his mother's laughter.

Even as an adult, Clay was haunted during every rainstorm by his mother's funeral. He would always recall trying to stand at attention while water was gently streaming in at one corner of the grave just feet from where he stood, adding to the accumulation six feet below the ground. The night of the funeral, while sleeping, he dreamed that his mother was floating in her coffin, tiny bubbles emanating from her nose and mouth. The dream gave the distinct impression that she was drowning and the family had killed her when they allowed her to be placed in that sopping hole. It was a nightmare that haunted Clay many times over the next several years.

Nine years after the funeral, on the way to his own wedding, Clay had decided to get his car cleaned. It was a beautiful, bright, sunny day as his car was pulled along the track through the car wash. Water sprayed, brushes spun, and soap appeared and disappeared as cloth strips slapped across the windshield. Already dressed in his tuxedo, Clay was excitedly but also nervously thinking of the upcoming wedding to Jessie, the woman to whom he had given his heart. After the reception, they would leave in their shiny car and head to their hotel at the airport in Detroit. From there they would fly to Arizona for their honeymoon. However, when he emerged from the wash, it was raining so hard that he never saw the trashcan he plowed into, leaving a slight dent and a permanent yellow streak on his bumper. And moments later, when Clay pulled his muddied car into the church parking lot, he stepped in a water puddle up to his ankles as he exited his parked car. He endured the entire wedding and reception while his socks squished with each and every step.

Now here he was standing under the overhang at the grocery store with his son, Tanner, grocery bags in tow, but the car 45 yards away at the back of the lot. With no jacket or hat, there would be no escaping a soaking unless they waited the storm out.

Clay only remembered liking rain two times in his life. The first was when there was a rainstorm of epic proportions when he was a young boy living in Haslett, Michigan. His city street flooded and every kid in the neighborhood waded into the river that had developed between the sidewalks. Clay hadn't liked the storm much, but the end result was marvelous. To seven-year-old Clay, it was like having the mighty Mississippi in his own front yard. For a day and a half, he was Huck Finn skipping stones, fishing, or riding a steamboat past the banks of his own front yard. The second time he felt appreciation for rain was while pitching at a baseball game. Less than a month before, Clay had acknowledged with young teenaged certainty that he had special "powers" to influence the way people thought, but he had determined not to use those powers at this one particular game, and he was getting hit hard by the other team. Luckily for Clay, lightning, thunder, wind, and rain swept in, and a great storm caused the game to be cancelled in just the third inning. Clay was spared further frustration and humiliation. It was while sitting alone in his bedroom during that storm, at the age of just thirteen, that Clay began deliberating as to how he was to live out his unique existence. As far as he knew, he was the only one on the planet with his ability, and he wasn't sure if it was to be a blessing or a curse. At that time, the only thing he knew for sure was that he wasn't going to tell anyone about it even though he somehow knew that his silence would almost certainly haunt him the rest of his life.

"I hate when it rains," Tanner echoed his father's thoughts as he and his father sprinted through the parking lot, splashing puddles and dodging traffic as they went.

Clay couldn't help but wonder when his son would decide for himself what he liked or didn't like, knowing that when Tanner was seven years old and the Thomases were at a family reunion getting splattered by gusting sheets of rain, Clay had said, "I hate the rain and you do too." As Tanner locked onto his father's eyes, his mind was instantly and permanently manipulated. Clay felt immediate remorse when Tanner emphatically stated, "I hate the rain too." Tanner should have been allowed to make up his own mind, but Clay had been irritated with Jessie when she smiled and took in a deep breath while his plate flew away in a whirlwind and he realized that another car washing was being ruined. Clay had long since decided to give his son the opportunity to change his own mind, but he wondered if Tanner ever would.

Tanner was now 17 years old, a senior in high school. Just like his father, he had recovered from his own difficult childbirth. Clay liked to remind Tanner occasionally how he emerged from his mother's body in perfect shooting form, foreshadowing his awesome basketball career. In the hospital, Clay's father, Tanner's grandfather, had explained to the family that Clay had had a similarly traumatic childbirth with his mother in the ambulance. He too emerged nearly strangled to death and semi-conscious, paramedics applying emergency resuscitation techniques. Like with Clay, only time could tell what affect the trauma would or would not have on Tanner's brain. Fortunately, both father and son had grown up to lead normal, productive lives. At least Tanner had thus far. Clay could never quite see himself as "normal," not with his secret ability to control minds.

One time Tanner tried to actually pinpoint when it was that he had decided to hate rain. He thought that it was at a picnic before recalling that it was at that family reunion many years before. He remembered because a geeky boy with whom he supposedly shared a great-grandparent was in attendance, and the kid somehow managed to get attacked by a porcupine. Before the reunion meal commenced, a large number of family members were involved in a softball game. The nerdy second cousin, Tanner recalled, held the ball bat with his fists approximately five inches apart. There was no convincing him that this was not the correct way to hold a bat. When the pitch was slowly tossed in, he was standing on the right side of the plate, but he managed to take an aggressive left-handed swing, letting loose of the bat, which propelled into someone's grandfather behind the plate. Eventually, with his father's help, the boy finally made contact with a pitch and then proceeded to sprint exuberantly down the third-base line and into the outfield, where he grabbed a ball glove from a little girl and threw it out of play. When faced with rules and expectations for the game, the boy whined and complained so much that his father finally shooed him off, and he went exploring instead.

When Tanner's second cousin discovered a brownish-yellow colored porcupine cornered in some scrub brush near the woods, the timid animal turned its back to the boy, hiding its snout between its forelegs. There was nowhere for the mammal to run, so it simply raised its quills and waited. The boy zoologist correctly deduced that porcupines weren't aggressive animals, so he decided to make a pet of the prickly rodent. He grabbed at its rump with both hands, incorrectly deducing that the porcupine was willing to submit peacefully. He screamed bloody murder as a hundred or so of the 30,000 three-inch long quills ended up imbedding themselves in the boy's hands. The child's father tried to pull several of the barbs out, to no avail, so the parents hurried him into their parked Volvo and headed for the hospital. Then grace was said and the potluck dinner began.

Tanner recalled how proud he was of his father, who had hit two extremely long home runs in the softball game, and he was pressed up closely to his dad at the picnic table. The food was fantastic. His father was enthusiastically eating some strawberry-rhubarb pie for dessert when the dark clouds rapidly rolled in. There was a rather close bolt of lightning followed by a tremendous peal of thunder. Then Clay's plate, pie and all, was torn from his hand, the wind carrying an amazing torrent of rain that splashed down on the pavilion. Tanner remembered his mother, Jessie, smile a glorious smile and Tanner, who liked the smell of rain, inhaled a deep breath of the humid air. He thought it was funny watching people scrambling for cover under the pavilion and at the same time was enjoying the refreshment and coolness that the sudden storm brought. And then all at once, after looking into his father's frustrated eyes, Tanner decided that he hated rain and an irrational anger welled up inside him.

***

Jessie had wanted lots of kids—well, at least four or five. Clay had been a high school math teacher, working diligently on his Master's degree in math while also coaching the school's varsity baseball team; Jessie worked as a medical assistant for a successful pediatrician in town. They loved kids and believed they'd be great parents. But after the birth and ensuing surgery, Jessie and Clay had to settle for just one child. Jessie had figured it was her responsibility to furnish Clay with the whole starting infield for his high school baseball team, but that was not to be so. Clay often thought of how he had *made* her believe she wasn't at fault and forget about the events of that fateful day, and then he justified his actions by telling himself that he did the right thing for the woman he loved because she needed to be happy and to snap out of her despairing thoughts. From the moment Clay had met Jessie, he knew that he would choose to love her for the rest of his life, but he also decided that he wouldn't make her love him back, nor would he take away any of her other choices in life. At that moment in the hospital, he had broken his promise to himself to never control Jessie's mind, and he had taken away her own right to sort out her own emotions and deal with her guilt in her own way. It was what Clay had decided was best for her, but it left him to somehow feel *he* was deserving of blame and to feel even more determined to never manipulate her mind again.

It seemed to Clay at the time that he had done what was best for his family, but Jessie always seemed to have a lingering guilt that she didn't understand. Clay knew that there continued to be things about her that she would never share with him, almost as if she sensed that there were things about her husband that he would always hide from her. He never really felt completely confident that she loved him, but he took great comfort in knowing that he had never influenced her love. Clay also took great satisfaction in the knowledge that Jessie had been a fantastic mother from the very beginning. Tanner became an honor student, a superior athlete, captain of the football, basketball, and baseball teams even as a junior, and though Clay sometimes felt he had less control of Tanner's behavior than he would like, he was very proud of his son. He was a mature, handsome, talented teenaged boy who people seemed to like. Clay loved his son, but it was to his wife that Clay gave most of the credit for his development. It was like she gave her one child the love she had planned for four or five.

Loving the Rain

Jessie Thomas was a smorgasbord of emotions. She was as volatile as a volcanic eruption, except, with her, the eruptions weren't necessarily always fiery. She could get angry easily, cry easily, or easily jump to erratic conclusions. But she could also laugh easily and get exuberantly excited. She could be the life of a party, never worried about embarrassing herself. She was able to laugh at herself, and seemingly all people loved her. She was, well, unpredictable. Unfortunately for Jessie, she was not one of the seventy-five percent or so of hysterectomy patients that are cured of PMS, so for about one-fourth of each month, she was *extra* unpredictable and even more emotional, and Clay and Tanner had learned to steer clear of her. Jessie was smiling now, however. It was raining—raining hard. It was a mid-August afternoon. The grass was dry and browning, and she was having trouble keeping her flowers perky ever since the worst summer temperatures had arrived, but this precipitation was sure to help. She loved the rain. She never could understand why her husband and son couldn't see how wonderful it was. Of course, she'd heard Clay's stories about nightmares concerning his mother, and she remembered how much the storm on their wedding day had bothered him, so she cut him some slack, but why did rain make Tanner such an angry sourpuss?

She remembered the family reunion when Tanner got all red in the face, clenched his fists, and proclaimed that he hated rain just like his dad. She remembered her father-in-law, Mr. Thomas, who always said grace at the reunions, turning his ankle when he stepped sideways off the cement platform under the pavilion while praying for the food. He was praying, then without warning, there was a thudding noise and when Jessie looked up, Clay's dad had fallen from sight. He picked himself off from the ground, dead grass and dirt clinging to his shoulders and back, and a squashed olive on the side of his face. He was only slightly embarrassed when he said, "God bless it...the *food* I mean. Dig in everyone!" There were a few embarrassed giggles and then finally laughter erupted and the reunion continued in good spirits—until the abrupt rainstorm, that is. And it was during that storm that Tanner

23

announced his loathing for rain, a tremendous disappointment for Jessie, who loved it.

***

Jessie Thomas was gorgeous—tall, with long, athletic legs and a nearly perfect figure; big, sparkling green eyes that could get a smile from anyone; and full lips covering perfectly white teeth. Gorgeous strawberry-blond hair outlined a stunning, tanned face. Clay recognized that it was difficult for people to keep their eyes off Jessie. He believed that because she was physically so perfect-looking, people were extra-willing to overlook the negative side of her emotions. Clay had figured from the beginning that she was out of his league, so he was especially grateful to have her—about three-fourths of each month.

As for Clay, he seemed to have a lot going for him. He had just turned 40 and was still fit, showing no signs of graying or balding. He was an intelligent man, kind of logical in his thinking, with brown hair and eyes, and a smile that could light up his face if and when he could find something to smile about. He would smile when Jessie was happy, and he would smile when Tanner pleased him, but more often than not he seemed distant, and that distance had been wearing on his wife for years. He was actually a cup-half-full kind of person, who tried to see the good in everyone and in every situation, but the longer he lived alone with his secrets, the lonelier he felt. Clay had always been a good athlete, and he did his best to be a good teacher and coach who worked harder than most people were willing. He was a good family man who provided for his family's material and personal needs, and he was on his way up as a teacher and coach, having accepted a professor's position at Mott Community College where he was also coaching the varsity baseball team. There were rumors that some larger universities were looking at him to become their next coach. But there *was* something wrong with Clay. He could *make* people think whatever he wanted them to think, as long as he looked them in the eyes, so he often would not look them in the eyes, and it made him look to Jessie and sometimes to others that he lacked confidence. Lack of confidence was actually the farthest

24

thing from the truth, however, because Clay knew that he could get anything he wanted out of life; he was very confident about that. But he also knew that using his "powers" to get what he wanted left him unhappy and unfulfilled, which was what was *really* wrong with Clay—that and his loneliness. He had managed to always keep his secrets to himself. Clay loved Jessie very much, and thus far Jessie had chosen to stick with Clay, but Clay could not help but fear that someday she would learn his secrets and things would be different.

Jeff La Ferney

Chapter 2

When Clay and Tanner arrived home, hair matted down and shirts and shoes soaked from their run through the parking lot, Jessie was on a swing on the porch, sitting and thinking. She had been mulling over a conversation with Clay several months before...

"There's a guy where I work out that's been flirting with me, Clay."

"Is that right? Did you tell him to stop...that you're happily married?"

"No, it's innocent. Do you think I should tell him to stop?"

"If that's what you want, Jessie. It's up to you."

"So if I don't want him to stop, it's okay with you that another man is flirting with me?"

"I don't like it, but it's not *my* decision to make. It's yours."

Jessie was in one of those moods of which Clay could never predict and be prepared. She was immediately irritated. "Clay, I made that up. There's no guy; there's no flirting. I just wanted to see if you cared. You really don't care, do you?"

...Jessie did her best thinking in the rain. As was happening more and more of late, she was becoming determined to find satisfaction in her life, satisfaction that her husband wasn't delivering.

Clay and Tanner hauled the groceries from the car and put them on the kitchen counter. Clay unpacked them and put them away before heading to the porch to talk with Jessie. Tanner, cell-phone in hand, thumbs texting away, escaped work the first chance he had and went off to his room for more privacy.

"Hey, Jess. Quite a rain we're getting, isn't it?"

"We need it."

"You didn't sleep well last night. You feeling okay?'

"Fine, Clay. I'm always fine." She was staring out into the steady shower as she spoke.

"Bad dreams? Stress at work?"

"No, just things on my mind, I guess."

"Wanna talk about it?"

"No, it's nothing." She needed to change the topic, so she asked, "Has the rain messed up your plans for the day?"

"I'm still leavin' in about half an hour. The rain's already letting up here, and it's heading to the North. We're golfing at Sugarbush in Davison." Clay was planning on playing 18 holes with some other instructors and coaches from Mott Community College in a fundraiser scramble for the baseball and softball teams. For what was the second time, he asked Jessie, "You sure you don't want to come and help out in the clubhouse?"

To Clay, she seemed a little distracted when she replied, "No, I told you I'd rather not. I'll be fine here. I've got errands to run, and I like the idea of a little time to myself. You know that Tanner's got plans with friends, right? Swimming and a bon fire."

"Yeah, he told me. Well, I'm gonna grab my golf gear and maybe get a bite to eat before I leave. Want anything?"

"No…thanks, I'm fine."

She didn't seem "fine" to Clay, but he had an obligation to his baseball program, and though he had the mind powers to do it, he wasn't about to make her talk if she didn't want to. He threw on a Mott Community College baseball shirt and hat, feeling the strain once again of the temptation to control her mind and the sadness of the knowledge that he had a gift that he felt he couldn't use. There was an uncertainty developing in his marriage that once again brought on the inescapable feeling of loneliness. The person he was closest to was actually very far away, and yet Clay felt powerless to do anything about it. He grabbed his golf shoes and clubs and a rain jacket. He then made up a couple of sandwiches for lunch. The rain was slowing down, but Jessie was still sitting on the porch watching the drizzle when Clay was ready to go. He leaned down and kissed her.

He felt the urge to stay home and talk, to be the husband that he wanted to be, but he had a responsibility to live up to, so instead he said, "You sure you're okay? Do you want me to call this afternoon?"

"No. I'm fine," she said again, sounding a little irritated with the question. "Just call so I know when you'll be home, and have fun," she added with a little half smile.

"Since when is a fundraiser fun?" Clay rolled his eyes a bit and smiled. "Maybe my team will win a trophy. See ya."

Jessie carefully watched as her husband drove down the street. She pulled out her new cell phone, the prepaid TracFone that she purchased earlier in the week. She had actually hoped that somehow Clay would have changed his plans and she wouldn't be making the call, but when his car turned at the street corner, she punched in the number.

"Hello."

"Hi, Tony. It's Jessie."

"I'm glad you called. The rain had me a little worried."

"My husband just left and should be gone most of the day. My son'll be gone all day too. Have you made plans for us?"

"Well, you could come over to *my* place…a little lunch, then who knows what could happen after that?"

"I've told you that I'm not willing to do anything like that. You have a plan B?"

Tony smiled, "Um, I could come to *your* place…a little lunch, then who knows after that?"

"How 'bout a plan C?" Jessie tried to sound irritated, but in reality, she liked the flirting quite a bit.

"Plan C is I've got two tickets on an Amtrak to Port Huron. We can talk, walk around the port and look at some boats we can only *dream* of owning, and then take the train back long before dark. How's that sound?"

"Much better. I'm actually willing to try plan C. Which station?" Jessie asked.

"Lapeer. 1:35 departure time. Hopefully the rain'll stop."

"It's already slowing down. I'll be there early. See ya soon."

Jessie snapped the phone shut and slid it back in her pocket. She was going to meet Tony Blanchard, a 26 year old medical intern that she had met at the pediatric clinic. He had finished all but one final rotation and had somehow ended up at the clinic instead of the hospital, working with Jessie and Dr. Hogue for several weeks. He had been flirting and then hitting on Jessie from day one, and his four-week rotation would be coming to a close in the next few days. Jessie finally agreed to the "date" after seeing him outside of the office on two other occasions, just sitting together in a car and talking. She enjoyed his conversations and the excitement the meetings had provided. Besides Tanner's sporting events, her life was clearly lacking excitement. She didn't have a clue what she was doing, but she knew she was searching for something. What would be the harm in a little fun? So while Clay would be playing golf and raising money for his baseball program, Jessie would be on a date to Port Huron.

"I'm heading out, Mom," Tanner announced. "I'll be at Mike Powell's."

"When'll you be home?"

"After the pool party, there's a bonfire. Football starts Monday, so it's kind of an end-of-the-summer bash for us football players, but I'll be home by midnight."

"Have fun...be good," Jessie added ironically.

As soon as Tanner left the house, Jessie began changing, and the same anticipation, excitement, and fear that kept her awake most of the night returned.

***

The following Thursday, while Tanner was at football two-a-days, Clay was at a meeting at the college, and Dr. Hogue was on the golf course with Tony Blanchard, Jessie was at lunch with her best friend, Carlee Simpson, at Applebee's. Jessie was determinedly poking her way through a Paradise Chicken Salad. Her attention was first riveted upon the pico de gallo that she spread across her salad greens and then grimly focused upon the chunks of pineapple, mandarin oranges, apple, and blackened grilled chicken she was spearing with her fork. Carlee seemed less transfixed on her Grilled Shrimp and Spinach Salad, so she reestablished the conversation.

"Did you say how the family is doing?" Carlee asked, breaking Jessie out of her food trance. Carlee knew the *real* conversation would begin soon enough.

"Everyone's fine. Clay's gearing up for the beginning of the fall term in early September and for fall baseball. Tanner's practicing football twice a day. He has a game the Thursday before Labor Day. How're Mark and the girls?"

"The girls are in shopping-for-school mode. Angela has cheerleading and Heather has tennis. Mark is currently repairing the couch."

"What'd he do this time?"

"Okay. There was a light bulb out on our ceiling fan. He couldn't reach it with a chair, so instead of getting a ladder, he decided to stand on the back of the couch, which, of course, tipped over. Miraculously the couch survived the tumble, but Mark fell forward and while trying to catch himself on one of the couch legs, he snapped it cleanly off. There's no telling what kind of damage he'll do trying to fix it." The women laughed as they continued to poke away at their salads.

"So your Tony's a golfer?" Carlee asked, finally getting to the meat of the conversation.

"Enough small talk, huh? Get right to it?"

"What're friends for? No sense beating around the bush."

"Okay…no, he's not a golfer, but Dr. Hogue is, so he's along for the free ride. And he's not 'my' Tony. What else do you want to know?"

"What happened Saturday?"

Jessie outlined the train trip, the lunch, and the walk around Port Huron. She explained where Clay and Tanner were and how the plans were made.

"And then…?" Carlee asked.

"And then I got back in my car at the station in Lapeer and drove home."

"I'm hoping that nothing happened."

"If you mean physically, no. Well, almost no. We held hands a little, and he kissed me *after* I got in my car, so it wasn't much of a kiss." She then explained how she made it home long before either family member returned.

"Will you see him again?"

"I don't think so. It was exciting, though…scary actually. I have to admit it. But Tony's rotation is complete and he'll be moving on. I just did it out of curiosity. I like how he treats me."

"Flirts with you, you mean."

"Yeah, I like it. He notices everything about me. He bought me a bracelet because he said he's never seen me wear one. I've been wearing it for five days, and Clay has yet to notice it. Clay will compliment me once in a while, but Tony flatters me."

"He flatters you because he wants something from you. You *do* realize that, right?"

"Sure. He wants to sleep with me; that's flattering too."

"I don't recommend you do it."

"I won't. It pretty much has to be over. We talked about it a bit. But I sure liked the excitement."

"You be careful, Jessie. There're some pretty rotten guys in the world. You're married to one of the good ones."

"If he's so good, why do I always feel like he's hiding something from me? Maybe *he's* the one who's having an affair."

"I don't believe that and neither do you. What's really wrong?"

"Let me give you an example. About six or eight weeks ago, I got all dressed up, put on my make-up, did my hair, put on perfume. Then I told Clay I was going out. He asked me where, and I said, 'Out.' He asked me who I was going with and I said, 'Just some friends, Clay, okay?' He said okay, and he looked away like he always does, like he's ashamed or something. I asked him if he'd rather I stayed home and did something with him, and he said, 'I want you to do whatever you'd like.' So I said I'd like to go out with my friends."

"Where'd you go?"

"Funny you should ask, because Clay never did. I sat in my car and cried. I wasn't going anywhere; I just wanted to see if he even cared." Jessie picked at some more fruit slices and a bite of chicken. "He seems so unhappy, Carlee. And my life is in such a rut. He loves me...I know that. He tells me all the time, and he really is kind and caring to me, but I swear he's drifting farther and farther away from me, and I'm bored with the whole thing."

"So this Tony brought you excitement, and you think that's what your life needs?"

"Maybe...and maybe not..."

"Well, I know from experience that whatever you do outside of Clay is *not* going to work out. You have a good man, Jessie. You'd better figure out what it is you need before you make a mistake that you regret. Whatever you decide, though, I'll be here for you."

Jeff La Ferney

Chapter 3

It was a beautiful fall evening, mid-October. Clay and Jessie were watching Tanner's Friday night football game with Jessie's parents and about 2,000 other fans. Jessie's eyes were scanning the crowd for one face in particular, and when she saw it, she gave a smile of satisfaction. John, her newest secret interest, had come to the game simply to see her. He would watch her closely and they would find a way to run into each other somehow; maybe she'd make a trip to the restroom or concession stand. The thought of talking to John again, even for just a couple of minutes, was very exciting.

The game was away, at Ortonville-Brandon High School, a school about 22 miles southeast of where Kearsley High School was located in Flint, Michigan. Ortonville had a wonderful new facility that included artificial field turf. It was a low-scoring game—7-7 at halftime. When the horn sounded, Jessie slipped away on the pretense of heading for the restroom, and just as she expected, John slid in beside her and lightly gripped her arm. A shockwave of pleasure followed immediately. "I was hoping you'd get away sometime during the game."

"I only have a couple of minutes before I have to head back. My parents are up there with Clay. It's really nice to see you, though."

"I came just for you. The game's boring, but I've enjoyed watching you. Are we on for tomorrow?"

Jessie had been communicating with John for quite a few weeks, since a short time after her date and "separation" from Tony. *This* relationship seemed to hold more promise. He was a man much closer in age, who had the same concerns about discretion. He seemed to understand Jessie's situation much better than Tony had, and he'd been very mature and kind. "It looks good. I'll call you as soon as I get a chance. Thanks for coming." He smiled the kindest, friendliest smile, and Jessie headed back to her seat. She felt a twinge of guilt, especially as she wondered how disappointed her parents would be if they knew what she was doing. But on the other hand, it'd been almost two months since her talk with Carlee, and her relationship with Clay hadn't improved at all. Clay seemed more preoccupied than ever. A couple of times, he had looked Jessie in the eyes, and she felt that long-lost tingling of excitement. He seemed ready to open up to her, but then he'd have second thoughts. He'd kiss her lightly, say "I love you," and go back to his isolated loneliness. John wasn't like that. He knew how to talk and listen and was always willing to share his feelings. Jessie really liked John, and she smiled, thinking of what was planned for the next day.

The score remained close in the second half and was just 10-9 at the end of the third quarter. Brandon had kicked a field goal and then Kearsley scored a safety on the last play of the quarter when Brandon's long snapper let loose of a magnificent snap that ricocheted off the goalpost crossbar and then off the back of the head of the leaping punter. Somehow the punter regained his senses enough to shove the ball out of the back of the end zone before a Kearsley player could recover it for a touchdown, but Kearsley was awarded two points for the safety and would receive the ball to start the fourth quarter. Brandon punted to the Hornets, and after a decent run back, Kearsley started their drive on their own 45 yard line. They managed just one first down when an eight-yard pass was completed to Tanner Thomas on third down with five yards to go. Junior quarterback Luke Simms's third down pass on the next series went incomplete, and Kearsley was forced to punt.

The Ortonville Trojans fielded the punt and proceeded to put together a very nice drive, culminating in a 31 yard field goal. With just under three minutes to play, the score was Brandon 13, Kearsley 9. Less than 30 seconds later, the Kearsley Hornets scored the go-ahead touchdown on a pass to Tanner. The stunned home crowd sat silently as the Kearsley faithful celebrated; yet, for some reason, Kearsley's coach was shouting at his quarterback. No one in the stands could understand what was happening, but Tanner knew...

It was second down and three yards to go on the Kearsley 47 yard line. Kearsley had run the kickoff all the way back to its own 40 yard line. Tanner's friend, Mike Powell, the tailback, had run seven yards up the middle and the clock was stopped at 2:37 because of an injury. The quarterback, Luke Simms, had just returned from the sideline with the next play.

"Okay, Coach says to run split right, 32 iso."

That meant the tight end would line up on the left while the receiver, Tanner, would split out wide on the right. The fullback would be the lead blocker, and Mike Powell would follow his block up the middle. The quarterback would roll to the right after the handoff, faking a run or a possible rollout pass. The play before, they had run the exact play and the cornerback had released Tanner to the safety and had stepped up, thinking the quarterback was running. Simms had made a couple of good runs earlier in the game. Tanner, however, was wide open on the play—the safety had come in on run support also. As Luke looked around the huddle, Tanner began to speak, focusing his eyes on Luke's. "If we run that play again, I'll be wide open again, but you won't have the ball. Luke, run 526 QB waggle. They'll think we're running, and I'll be wide open." The formations were the same for both plays, but 526 QB waggle had the quarterback faking the handoff and then rolling out to pass.

"Coach says to run split right, 32 iso."

By then the injured player, one hand holding his battered groin, was being helped off the field. The clock would be restarted soon. There wasn't much time left for discussion. Tanner refocused on Luke's eyes. "You should run 526 QB waggle. I'll be open. Run it, Luke."

Luke swallowed as if composing himself, and then he said, "526 QB waggle. On two."

As Luke prepared to bark off his signals, Tanner looked into the eyes of the cornerback, crouching into position. *"Go for the quarterback,"* Tanner thought. On the second "Hut," the fullback dove into the line; Luke faked a handoff to Mike Powell and rolled right. The cornerback dropped two steps back and then let Tanner run past just as before, and he began charging toward the quarterback. The safety fell for the fake and rushed forward to make a tackle, leaving Tanner wide open, just as he expected. Luke lofted a soft pass down the field which Tanner neatly grabbed and ran into the end zone for the go ahead score. The crowd erupted into an exuberant frenzy, but Coach Simms (yes, he was Luke's very own father) was in an even greater frenzy.

"Since when do you call your own plays, Luke? What in the heck were you thinking?"

"I just felt like calling it. I don't know."

"*Felt* like it!? Holy cow! What am *I* doing here, Luke? Maybe *you* should be the coach!"

"Why're you so upset, Dad? It worked; we scored."

"Shut up, Luke! You'd better hope we can hold them with all this *time* left on the clock, and then you'd better stay out of my sight when I get home tonight. You can't just be makin' up your own plays. Go sit down!"

Kearsley converted the extra point and the score was 16-13. On the bench, Tanner heard Luke say, "I don't know why I changed the play. All of a sudden it's what I wanted to do. My dad's ready to kill me."

…After the game, which Kearsley High managed to win, Tanner received his congratulations and slipped over to his parents before boarding the bus. Jessie was still looking for John and a chance to say goodbye. Jessie's mom and dad congratulated Tanner. They were coming over to the house, and Tanner was expected to be there. "I'm going out with some of the guys, Mom. I'll see you later. Thanks for coming, Grandma, Grandpa." Tanner leaned in for a hug from his grandmother.

"Not so fast, Tanner. You should come home for awhile," Clay responded.

"No, Dad. Mom," Tanner looked into her eyes, "tell him it's okay."

Jessie, who wasn't too focused on the conversation to begin with, responded to Tanner's request by saying, "It's okay. Don't worry, Clay. My parents see him all the time. Let him go."

Tanner had a little grin on his face that may have been because he just got one over on his mother and father or it may have been because his coach had just slapped Luke upside the helmet, which flew off his head and landed in a trash barrel. Coach Simms was yelling, "*I* call the audibles, Luke, not you!" Luke seemed unsure of himself as he pulled the helmet from the garbage. He looked directly at Tanner, and then stared out into space with some kind of far off look that seemed to indicate he couldn't quite figure something out. Clay shuddered momentarily because he recognized that look. Then in a moment of fatherly compassion, Coach Simms patted Luke on the butt and said, "Nice pass, son." He smiled and headed for the team bus.

Tanner winked at Luke and said, "See, everything's all right. He's proud of you, you know. It *was* a pretty good pass, Hero, but don't let it go to your head." Both boys then walked away to board the bus with smiles on their faces. As Clay observed, he could not shake the feeling that somehow Tanner had manipulated Jessie and maybe even had something to do with Luke calling plays that he wasn't supposed to call. Jessie seemed preoccupied with other thoughts and was paying no attention to the evening's unfolding events, but Clay had an anxious feeling about what he had just observed. He was going to have to keep a closer eye on Tanner.

Jeff La Ferney

Chapter 4

Jack Harding glared out his front window. There in the driveway was his son, Kevin, his daughter, TJ, and Tanner Thomas. Tanner had spent the night with Kevin after his football game, and he and Kevin were shooting baskets in the driveway. It irritated Jack to see TJ watching and teasing her boyfriend, and it irritated him doubly to see his son being friends with his biggest competition. When Jack didn't like something, he tended to do everything in his power to eliminate the problem, and he saw Tanner as a problem. Though very shady, Jack was a self-made, successful businessman. He tended to get what he wanted, and if someone was in his way, he eliminated the problem by whatever means necessary. After graduating from Okemos High School, Jack couldn't get away fast enough. He earned a degree in business, and after five years of mostly unethical scheming, Jack purchased an automobile salvage yard in Flint, Michigan, which he renamed Harding Metals. Since high school, Jack had been a bitter man, always blaming others for his failures and shortcomings and never really overcoming the disdain he had felt from his high school classmates. Approximately seven years after starting up his own business, the man he blamed the most, Clay Thomas, was offered the head baseball-coaching job at Mott Community College in Flint. There he would also teach a couple of math courses each semester. At the time, Jack had no idea that he was living in the same city with the one person he blamed the most for his worst memories.

Jack smiled to himself as he watched his son run off six consecutive long jump shots. He felt that Kevin was a star basketball player and that this, his senior year, would be the year that others would recognize his talent. But there in the driveway, rebounding for his son was his daughter's boyfriend, Tanner Thomas, the player that everyone else thought was the star of Kearsley's basketball team, and it angered Jack that his children were friends of Clay Thomas's son. Five years after Clay had taken the coaching job at Mott, Jack's ex-wife married a man who was to work and live in Toronto, Ontario. The marriage, another failure on Jack's resume, resulted in two remarkably good children, both of whom had to move in with their father because their custody arrangements wouldn't allow them to move out of the country. They were enrolled back into Kearsley Community Schools, where they had attended in early elementary school before the divorce. Kevin Harding ironically became a teammate of Clay's star son, Tanner, and TJ worshipped Tanner like a rock star groupie. Those two circumstances did nothing but draw the ire of Jack Harding, who hated Clay Thomas with a passion.

***

Jessie watched as Clay packed his things, said his goodbyes, and headed off for a day of watching Saturday baseball. There were a couple of ballplayers from the Detroit area that had contacted Clay about playing ball for Mott, whose reputation was growing year by year as a good place to play baseball. One was a big, scrappy, power-hitting catcher and the other a left-handed hitting first baseman, who was also purported to throw lefty at up to 90 miles per hour with a lot of movement. Clay was looking for recruits that fit the descriptions of both players, so he had decided to watch them play in an indoor baseball tournament at Total Sports Complex in Wixom, Michigan. Both players were Division 1 prospects whose grades concerned the major universities. A community college would be a good place to spend two years getting grades up before a transfer. If they were as good as advertised, Clay would be getting a couple of prizes.

Jessie relaxed as Clay pulled out of the driveway and headed away. Because Tanner had ended up spending the night with Kevin Harding after the football game, he also was not home. As long as the October weather stayed reasonably good, he was going to take his girlfriend, TJ, to a fair, which included a concert. He would be gone all day as well.

Jessie smiled as she considered the plans she had made with John. They were heading north to possibly Bay City or Midland, just to do a little shopping, have something to eat, and talk in a place where they weren't likely to be recognized. Jessie liked how John was going slow and not pressuring her in any way. She wasn't looking to have an affair; she was simply enjoying his company and the way he made her feel. She liked the compliments, the excitement, the way he didn't take her for granted. He was kind, generous, and most importantly for her, he seemed so self-assured and confident. It seemed to Jessie that Clay took her for granted and didn't notice things about her. He seemed to lack the confidence of John and didn't seem to take charge of things the way John did. John made her feel like she was special, while Clay made her feel frustrated. Her husband didn't get mad at her and never seemed jealous, but he gave in to her too easily. Did he even love her? It was hard for her to tell.

They met in a restaurant parking lot and John drove. He gave her a rose and a Hershey's chocolate bar. "You said it was your favorite."

"That's sweet. Thank you."

"I hope you don't mind that I took it upon myself to make plans."

"No, I like that. What're we doing?"

"We're going to Midland and we're visiting Dow Gardens. I know it's October and the flowers won't be at their best, but the weather's pretty nice today, and the fall leaves are beautiful. We can tour by ourselves and eat in the picnic area. If the weather takes a turn for the worse, we'll go out, but otherwise, I brought a picnic lunch."

"You're just trying to romance me, aren't you?"

"I don't see what's wrong with that. Can't get too much romance, if you ask me."

John always dressed nicely. He had dark hair, dark skin, and dark eyes. His somewhat crooked nose seemed to give him character. His eyes didn't smile often, but he seemed to always be smiling at Jessie, like he had something up his sleeve that he wasn't telling her about. He wasn't always clean-shaven, but he was cleanly shaved for the "date." She liked the way he paid attention to details and seemed genuinely interested in listening to her; he asked too many questions about her family, though, and considering what she was doing with him, those questions made her uncomfortable, so she would steer the conversation away. He was divorced, had two kids, and ran his own business.

"You have beautiful eyes...oh, I like that bracelet...you look a lot younger than 38...you're funny...smart...so pretty..." John was ready and willing to flatter Jessie, and Jessie liked it. She enjoyed her day with him very much, and when he dropped her off at her car, he opened her car door and simply kissed her hand like a gentleman. "Will I see you again, do you think?"

"Yes." She couldn't hold back her smile.

"Good. I had a great time with you."

"I did too. I'll call you soon, John. Goodnight."

***

As soon as she had the car in gear, Jessie was on the phone to Carlee. She had to talk to someone.

"Hi, Jess; I thought you'd never call. I was worried about you."

"There's nothing to worry about. It was perfect, Carlee. I really like him."

"Are you going to tell me who 'him' is?"

"Not yet."

"Are you *looking* for trouble, Jessie? Do you have any idea what you're doing?"

"We're just friends. He's been a perfect gentleman. Nothing has happened."

"So, are you going to tell Clay?"

44

"Of course not."

"Then something is happening; don't fool yourself."
***

When Clay returned, Jessie was preoccupied with her own thoughts and didn't seem to be listening to his description of the two excellent players he'd been watching all day. When Tanner returned, she didn't even bother to talk to him, something that was very unusual. She usually kept a close eye on the clock and couldn't wait to talk to Tanner about his day. Instead, she got in bed early, kissed Clay lightly on the lips, said goodnight, and rolled over on her side, her back to her husband who was going over his notes. She looked lovely as always and Clay thanked the Lord once again for his amazing luck in snagging Jessie. Maybe it was time he did something nice for her...to make sure she knew how he felt about her. She sure seemed down in the dumps.

Jeff La Ferney

Chapter 5

Clay had been in touch with several college coaches who were interested in watching Tanner play football. It was senior night, probably the last home game. Kearsley was 6-2 and guaranteed to have a playoff spot the following week, but a win against Holly might get them a home game in the districts. Coaches from Grand Valley State, Oakland University, and the University of Toledo suggested that they might be in attendance, so Clay was looking over the crowd when he spotted a Toledo sweatshirt worn by a man who was approaching the Thomas's seats. Clay got his attention and discovered it was Toledo's basketball coach, Sammy Moretti. Sammy shook hands with a firm handshake and sat down next to Clay. Sammy was a large, rugged-looking gentleman, but he was friendly from the start. He had salt and pepper hair, broad shoulders, and a thick neck like someone who spent considerable time in a weight room. His slightly protruding belly demonstrated that he was a man who also knew how to enjoy a good meal. He explained that he was from the Flint area, having gone to school at Davison High School before going off to play basketball for the University of Toledo. From there he became a graduate assistant, then sports information director, then recruiting coordinator and head defensive assistant, before finally getting the head coaching job two years back. He knew there was a lot of talent in the Flint area, so he came back occasionally to recruit and visit family; his parents still lived in Davison. He expressed interest in Tanner as a future point guard for his program and said he thought he'd take in a game to make that interest clear. He laughed, "But my mother's linguini with white clam sauce was reason enough to come. I sure do miss her cooking."

Tanner had the performance of his career. He caught eleven passes for 218 yards and three touchdowns. Nearly all of his yardage and all three of his touchdowns were in the first half alone. Tanner knew that some schools were there that were interested in him as a basketball prospect, so he was determined to make a good showing. Throughout the course of the football season, he was becoming more and more confident that he was able to somehow influence the minds of other people. He was in the heads of the Holly cornerbacks all night. Most of the time, they did just as Tanner told them. Sometimes they didn't, which confused Tanner somewhat, but he had drawn the conclusion that the more attention his opponents gave him and the more closely they eyed him, the more likely they were to respond to his mental suggestions. There were blown coverages, terrible mistakes going for Tanner's fakes, screaming coaches, shrugging shoulders, pointing fingers, replacement players, yet no one on Holly seemed to have much of a clue about what they were doing while defending Tanner. "It's like they think they know what he's doing and he keeps doing the opposite," Coach Moretti said at halftime after getting a bag of popcorn.

Like when I was pitching in junior high, Clay thought. He was becoming more certain than ever that Tanner was influencing everything that was happening.

***

Jessie was back to being her usual lovable self—jumping up and down and screaming, giving high-fives to everyone within reach, including quite a few gawking men who found a way to maneuver *within* her reach. After Tanner's second touchdown, when she threw her hands in the air, she sent her hot chocolate into orbit, the cup disappearing between rows of the bleachers. Before Tanner had scored his third touchdown, three different men had replaced her cup with another. It was a performance to remember—for both Tanner and Jessie—one that made Clay more

48

suspicious than ever about Tanner and happier than ever to be the one married to Jessie. Jessie enjoyed Tanner's performance, but she understood that she was also performing because John was at the game once again, keeping a very close eye on her. He seemed to be enjoying her antics as much as anyone. He always seemed to be smiling at her, even though his eyes at times seemed very cold. Jessie was having too much fun to figure that out, though, and she was enjoying Tanner's game very, very much.

Kearsley won easily and many of the starters, including Tanner, played very little in the second half. After the game, several recruiters hung around to introduce themselves and give congratulations. They gave cards with phone numbers and expressed their interest. Clay watched closely as Tanner shook hands and politely answered their questions. If the question was personal, however, he would avoid eye-contact and act as though the topic was not important to him—like he wasn't willing to give the topic too much of his attention.

The Hornets lost the next weekend in the first round of the playoffs to Lowell 38-10. Tanner bruised his thigh pretty badly in the first quarter, and though he attempted to play through it for awhile, it became obvious that Kearsley was not going to win the game, and Tanner sat out most of it. The football season was over. In the next two weeks before basketball practice began, Clay kept a very close eye on his son. By that time, he wasn't just suspicious that Tanner had the power to control minds; he was almost convinced of it. Memories of his childhood, when he began to recognize his powers, began to seep into his consciousness…

When Clay was ten years old, he had an encounter with a bear—not a real bear, a Chicago Bear. The Bears were playing an exhibition game at the 80,000 seat Pontiac Silverdome, and Clay's dad took him to the game. It was supposed to be "Autograph Night," but the Thomases were running a little late. Better than 60,000 fans were involved in various activities: using the restroom, buying refreshments or souvenirs, searching for seats. Many were still waiting for signatures—several players from the Chicago team were still signing autographs. The line for Walter Payton's signature was far too long and even journeyman quarterback Vince Evans was being overwhelmed with requests. But there was a linebacker by the name of Doug Buffone whose line was short enough to harbor the *possibility* that an autograph might be procured before the players headed back to the locker room or back to the playing field.

As Clay and his father worked their way into the line, Clay asked, "Who's Doug Buffoon?"

"Um, he's a linebacker, Son. Plays for the Bears."

"Isn't a buffoon some sort of a monkey?"

"I believe that would be 'baboon,'" Mr. Thomas said while stifling a smile.

"It's a funny name." Clay seemed especially interested in the topic of conversation. "What is a *buffoon*?"

"Well, it's kind of like a clown, I guess. Someone who, well, makes a fool of himself while trying to be funny. This man's name, though, is Buf-phone, I believe."

"Do you think he's nice?"

"Why do you ask?"

"'Cuz if he went to *my* school, everyone would call him 'Buffoon,' and I think that would make him mean."

Mr. Thomas regularly observed that his son thought things through a little more deeply than most ten-year-olds. He was also starting to perceive that they were running short of time and the likelihood of getting a signature was fading fast. Mr. Thomas wasn't the only perceptive Thomas, however. Clay realized that time was running short, but he also sensed that getting this autograph was more important to his dad than it was to himself. His dad would feel like he let his son down if they didn't manage to get at least one signature on "Autograph Night." Clay looked at the football player just as Doug Buffone looked up, and they made eye contact. Clay thought, *"Please give me an autograph."* The Bear's linebacker surprisingly stood and motioned for Clay to come forward.

When Clay got to the table, the linebacker said, "I only have a minute. Would you like an autograph?"

"Yes, please."

As he signed, Buffone asked, "Is that *all* you want?"

"Like what else?"

"How 'bout if I get a sack or an interception for you in tonight's game?"

"That's all right. I kind of want the Lions to have a chance."

Buffone laughed. "I knew when I laid eyes on you, you were a good kid. Enjoy the game."

As Buffone walked away, Clay said, "He *is* a nice man, Dad. I'm sure glad I don't have his name though."

Mr. Thomas laughed and said, "You should have asked for his jersey or wristbands or *something. I* think he'd have given you whatever you wanted."

Young Clay just shrugged and thought to himself, *"That wouldn't have been the right thing to do."*

When Clay looked back on his childhood, he pinpointed that encounter with Doug Buffone as probably the first time he'd controlled a person's mind. By the time he was 13, he had learned what he could do, and somehow he had also begun to learn that he needed to be careful and rarely use his powers. He could have made Doug Buffone act like a buffoon if he'd wanted to, or even a baboon if he knew what baboons acted like. But even as a ten-year-old, Clay didn't think that would be the right thing to do. He eventually determined that no one should know the power he possessed, so he kept it to himself and never told anyone...

That football game was 30 years ago. Clay had secretly lived with his powers for 30 years. At times, those years were remarkably frustrating and lonely. And as he evaluated his life, something that he had been doing a lot since he became suspicious that his son might have the same power, he felt that his most important relationships were less than fulfilling as well. He wasn't the husband or the father that we wanted to be. So he had finally decided it was time to share the secret with someone, maybe not Tanner just yet, and certainly not Jessie, but there were some things that needed to be discussed, and the sooner the better. He needed to sort out what to do before Tanner did something they both regretted.

Chapter 6

Pete Piggott *was* a buffoon. He was also the boys' varsity basketball coach at Kearsley High School. He was not a teacher. He was approximately 5'6", maybe 250 pounds. When seated, he had to lean back and then propel his head forward over his bulging waist to get enough momentum to stand. He had such tiny, meaty, sweaty hands that he couldn't get a good grip on a handshake, leaving whomever it was that he met to feel as if he or she was squeezing a small, wet guinea pig. The handshake didn't inspire much confidence, nor did his beady black eyes which were always on the move, searching for something that they never seemed to find and avoiding whomever it was that had just released the disgusting "guinea pig" and was wiping his or her hand off on the nearest article of clothing. He hurled insults at his players, blamed everyone else when things went wrong, was apt to have tremendous and often hilariously embarrassing temper tantrums, and somehow managed to win more games than he lost. The only real relationship he had with any known human being was a cousin in the area who took pity on him. The players just called him Pig or the Pigman—respectfully, of course.

Rumor had it that Piggott had spent time in jail for assaulting a paperboy in Missouri who brained Piggott with a throw from the street. Logical minds believed he probably hadn't committed a felony or the school district wouldn't have hired him, but practically everyone believed there was some truth to the story. Piggott worked security for Harding Metals, Jack Harding's Flint-area scrap yard specializing in the buying and selling of scrap metal, machinery, electrical supplies, and auto parts, among other things. Piggott guarded the junk and supposedly chased off the homeless and any would-be thieves and vandals. No one could even fathom that he once played the game himself, but he claimed to have been an all-conference point guard for Cass City in the early '70's. "I was thin, quick, and didn't sweat as much," he once said at a meet-the-team, demonstrating the only hint of humor he'd ever shared. Jack Harding's son, Kevin, would be a senior guard on Piggott's Kearsley basketball team. Pete Piggott didn't seem to really like anyone, except possibly Kevin Harding, but even with Kevin it was hard to tell for sure. The truth was that Piggott resented Jack so much that he actually felt compassion for his son. Coach Piggott wasn't married but was rumored to frequent many of the area "Gentleman's Clubs" in search of a certain dancer that he had his heart set on marrying. The story is that the dancer, a Miss Honey Suckle, had fled to Canada.

***

Like every typical high school boy, Tanner wasn't very motivated by the ringing telephone. "Get the phone!" Jessie yelled. It was Saturday afternoon, the weekend before basketball practices were to begin.

Tanner casually lumbered over to the phone and snatched it off the cradle on approximately the eighth ring. He said, "Hello," just as Jessie stormed out of her bedroom with some kind of gook on her face.

"Tanner, this is Coach Piggott," Piggott boomed into the phone.

"It's for me, Mom! Hey, Coach." Jessie shook her head, scowled at her son, and went back to whatever it was that she was doing to her face. Clay was outside, moving the snow blower from the shed into the garage, getting ready for winter.

"Just letting you know we're practicing at midnight Sunday. Midnight Madness."

"We have school on Monday, Coach." Though he knew it would do no good, Tanner was still hoping to change his coach's mind. The season before, during middle-of-the-night practice, the Pigman got so angry that he kicked a ball to the ceiling. It smashed against one of the hanging lights, knocking it out of its bracket. The safety chain unfortunately was unhooked and the huge light fixture fell to the floor, less than a foot from killing one of the players. Glass and metal flew everywhere. Two players cut themselves during cleanup, sending Piggott into a tizzy. "I ain't doin' no stinkin' paperwork! Friggin' injury reports! If you're still bleedin' by the time we get this cleaned up, you're cut!" No pun was intended—a line like that would have been too clever for the raving lunatic. The Pigman, who didn't seem to learn lessons like most moderately intelligent people did, later in another fit, hurled a basketball against the wall. This time it hit the fire alarm, breaking the glass and setting the alarms ringing. Practice ended when the firemen and the school superintendent showed up. Piggott left the gym, rubbing his reinjured, chronically sore rotator cuff. Both injured players, by the way, bandages still on their fingers two days later, got cut anyway.

"Take a nap, Thomas."

"I have a bruised thigh, Coach. I could use a few more days' rest."

"Kevin Harding would love to be point guard, Thomas. Rest in the off-season. I'll see you midnight Sunday. Be early." And he hung up.

Piggott loved midnight madness. He was used to working third shift, so the hours made no difference to him. And it didn't matter to him in the slightest that it was a school night. What he loved was that he could tell Jack Harding that he wouldn't be coming in to work. Jack could find someone else to post guard over his shady business dealings—shady in the sense that Jack was a criminal. He was a small-time criminal, but a criminal nonetheless. He fenced a few stolen items here and there and dabbled in money laundering, gambling, loan sharking, and was making a nice profit on the illegal sale of firearms. Harding Metals was reasonably legit, but that was daytime business. It was the nighttime business that Jack Harding lived for…that and his son,

Kevin, who Jack thought was a fine basketball player. Finer, of course, than he really was, but Jack hadn't seemed to notice his shortcomings over the years. He also had Pete Piggott in his back pocket. Pete Piggott worked security at Harding Metals so that if need be Jack could blackmail the coach and thereby expand his criminal activities by one. Jack looked at it as diversifying.

***

"You ready for practice?" Jack Harding asked his son on Sunday evening as Jack was preparing to head to the junkyard for another night of shady dealings and Kevin was packing shoes and Gatorade into a bag. Jack was a decent-looking man, slightly over six feet, muscular build, black hair, and a short, neatly trimmed goatee that he felt was an important amenity when doing business with the criminal types he often found himself dealing with. He would occasionally shave to impress "respectable" people. His bushy eyebrows hid his eyes a bit—eyes that always seemed suspicious or angry but never happy. He made a habit of wearing a suit and tie, even at Harding Metals, because it made him look more important than he really was. On his tie was a picture of a car crusher and a smashed vehicle the size of a small dresser.

"Yeah, I guess," replied Kevin.

"You gonna win the point guard job this year?"

"No. Tanner Thomas is the point guard." Kevin, at times, had more common sense than his father.

"You're better than him. I'll have to talk with that moron coach of yours to make sure you get the spot."

"Dad, Tanner is better than me."

"No he isn't. You made all-conference last year."

"I made honorable mention. Tanner made first-team. Tanner averaged more than 17 points a game. I averaged almost eight. I'll start, but *not* at point guard. Leave Coach alone, okay?"

"If he put you at the point, *you'd* be first-team."

"Probably not, but thanks for saying so. I'll see you tomorrow." Kevin exited the house, no more excited about practice than Tanner was. He was thinking of the time last year when the Pigman got so crazy he started blowing his whistle uncontrollably.

56

His cheeks were completely puffed out and his face was beet-red and sweating, yet he continued to blow the whistle until he literally passed out. Kevin remembered Mike Powell remarking, "If Piggott needs mouth-to-mouth, I think he's gonna die." Kevin laughed to himself, but it really wasn't a "good" memory. Something bad almost always happened in Piggott's practices.

***

Though Jack Harding had a daughter, he cared more about his son because it was through his son that he relived the sports career that he always felt was stifled by idiot teammates, bad breaks, and retarded coaches. Jack vowed that Pete Piggott was not going to stand in the way of Kevin's success. Harding first met Pete Piggott about 11 years previously. Pete wasn't as fat then, but he was still quite round and stupid looking. He was unemployed at the time and living in a small house in a neighborhood known as "Little Missouri" on the southeast side of Flint. Jack, who had dabbled in the bail bonds business (before switching to the more lucrative loan sharking business), got a call to bail Pete Piggott out of jail. Pete's angry and nearly incoherent story had something to do with hurting his shoulder and returning newspapers to their rightful and "bleeping owner."

Pete, being unemployed and barely literate, was unwilling to pay for the daily *Flint Journal* newspaper delivery. The newsboy, however, was getting his kicks out of irritating his non-customer, so he kept delivering even after Piggott made it *very* clear that he wasn't paying. He told Piggott that newspaper articles were written at the third grade reading level, so if he read carefully, it was possible that he could understand a few of the shorter ones. The newsboy would fold the paper into thirds, as he did his regular newspapers, but for Pete Piggott, he would fold the top and bottom into additional thirds, leaving it in an approximate four-inch by four-inch block. He would then bundle the brick securely with several rubber bands and fire it into Piggott's screen door with amazing speed and accuracy. Piggott would holler and scream and even occasionally throw one back, one time connecting with his attractive neighbor who was walking her dog. When she threatened to sue him, he decided that he had finally had enough. After drinking half a bottle of Jack Daniels and stomping around his house in anger, he finally summoned his courage and gathered his unread *Flint Journals* into a large burlap bag. Staggering each step of the way, he managed to drag them to the newsboy's home and started firing the newspapers back at the kid's front door. He stood in the street and screamed, threatened, and carried on while chugging the other half of the bottle of whisky. By the time he was nearly done with his pile, he had torn his rotator cuff and had been arrested for drunk and disorderly conduct. While Police Officer Lance Hutchinson hooked a handcuff around Piggott's left wrist, Pete's last throw glanced harmlessly off a shrub. He had managed to connect with the house just five times in nearly 40 attempts. Jack Harding agreed to post the 1,000 dollars needed to free Pete from jail, the surety bond to be paid back at 15 percent interest after Jack appeared in court.

In the trial, which should have resulted in a simple misdemeanor, Piggott ignorantly represented himself, and after several warnings to control his temper, he was finally cited with criminal contempt of court when he snatched the judge's gavel from her hand and fired it across the courtroom at the teenaged newsboy. The gavel sailed harmlessly into the wall while Piggott fell to his knees in rotator-cuff-induced pain. He was sent to jail for three days before being found guilty of drunk and disorderly conduct. He was fined 200 dollars and sentenced to 200 hours of community service. Piggott first volunteered his time at the Flint YMCA, coaching basketball, and eventually as an AAU coach. He realized that coaching was the only "job" he'd ever done that he was actually decent at, so when Kearsley High School needed to fill its vacated head boys basketball coaching position the day before the 2001-02 season began, Pete Piggott, the only applicant, became a varsity coach.

After the trial, Jack Harding had hired Piggott to guard his junkyard from any potential unruly elements such as thieves, vandals, and the homeless. Piggott owed Harding 150 dollars and the court 200 dollars, so he took the job against his better judgment—he rather didn't like the idea of working. Harding, for his part, figured the job took very little brains, and since his "business" was evolving more and more toward the criminal element, he figured Piggott could watch the place at night and never figure out what was going on. Kevin Harding was six at the time of the hiring, just about a year before his parents' divorce. As fate would have it, he had moved back into his father's home and would be a second-year varsity starter on Piggott's basketball team. Since Jack Harding "owned" Pete Piggott, he was sure that he could convince the coach to move his son to point guard so that he would get the attention and recognition that Tanner Thomas was getting.

Jeff La Ferney

Chapter 7

Midnight Madness was exactly that—madness. Tanner's leg was dragging as he gulped Gatorade from a bottle. Piggott was driving them like a madman, only this year he was being very careful not to break anything, so he hadn't thrown or kicked a ball yet. He *had* missed his mouth with a bottle of Gatorade. He was yelling at a couple of juniors, "This ain't little league any more. This is the big time an' time for you momma's boys to figure it out!" He was blathering on when he lifted his bottle for a drink; he missed his mouth completely, however, and splashed half its orange contents over his shirt. The juniors weren't smart enough to keep their laughter to themselves, so the coach had his team line up again for more sprints.

It was 2:30 AM, and Piggott was threatening them with more running. Midnight Madness was Coach Piggott's way of making a first impression, like a strict teacher who loosens up as the year goes along, except the Pigman never really loosened up. School would start at 7:30, and they would be back in the gym practicing again immediately after it ended. The players were tired and practice was long past being productive.

Tanner, during the last several weeks, had reached the conclusion that somehow he was able to influence what people were thinking. He could manipulate their minds, and they would do what he wanted them to do. It could not simply be a coincidence. Occasionally it didn't work, however, so even if he had considered sharing his conclusion with anyone, there wasn't enough evidence of "mind powers" to do so. And though he didn't know for sure why sometimes it didn't work, he was confident that it did work quite often, and he felt certain that his use of this power, once he could control it, could be very advantageous. Yet the more he thought about it, the more convinced he was that he should never share the knowledge of his ability with anyone because people would begin to suspect he was manipulating their every thought, and he couldn't imagine anyone would be happy about that, including himself. After a parent/teacher conference a little over a year ago, his psychology teacher remarked to Tanner, "Your dad loves you, but he seems like a lonely man...what's up with that?" Tanner couldn't help but wonder if he chose to hide his mind-control ability from everyone his entire life, would he end up lonely too?

But now it was 2:30 in the morning, and someone needed to stop Coach Piggott or there was soon going to be a mutiny. Tanner had been sending thoughts Pig's way for the past hour, but the beady-eyed man seemed immune. Eyes darting every which way, Tanner couldn't seem to get his attention, and Tanner couldn't say out loud what he was thinking for fear that the Pigman would line them up and run them again.

Piggott barked out Thomas's name, signaling to everyone that the drink break was over. It was time to get back to the madness. Tanner grimaced as he slowly walked over to his coach. "I noticed you were limping. What in the heck's wrong, you big sissy?"

"I told you yesterday that I had a thigh bruise from football. I'll be all right."

"You'd better believe you'll be all right, or I'll have you on the bench watchin' Harding run this team!"

Piggott's darting eyes landed on Tanner's for an instant and Tanner thought, *It's time for practice to end. Before someone gets hurt or quits.*

Piggott blinked and said, "Okay, Ladies, it's time for practice to end. Don't want any of you crybabies quittin' or gettin' hurt. Get some shut-eye and I'll see you after school." Piggott seemed confused as he checked his practice schedule then looked at his watch. He tilted his head while glancing at his team, then shrugged his shoulders and waddled off to his office. The team breathed a sigh of relief and headed for the locker room.

"What'o we got, five hours before school starts? Someone just wake me up before the warning bell." Mike Powell stretched out on a locker room bench as if he really might sleep there the rest of the night. "Good thing Piggy had a change of heart."

"Whatever you said, Tanner, thanks," Luke Simms chipped in.

"I didn't say anything. He asked me why I was limping; I reminded him about my leg and told him I'd be all right. Didn't say another thing."

"Then we're all as confused as him 'cause he *sure* looked confused after he stopped practice," Kevin Harding interjected. "I'm outta here." Kevin shut his locker, looped his bag over his shoulder, and never looked back. The others followed suit except Mike Powell who was already fast asleep, but nobody noticed. The first practice of the year, Midnight Madness, was done, and a whole season of madness waited.

Tanner's body was tired and his leg sore, but his mind was alert. Had he figured it out? Coach Piggott never seemed to look anyone in the eyes, including Tanner. Maybe that was why Tanner's thoughts were having no impact on him. When the Pigman finally made eye contact, Tanner finally got through to him. Limping across the parking lot, Tanner pulled his keys from his pocket and sighed a long sigh. His "powers" were coming into focus, but what was the point of it all? Should he tell someone? He didn't think so. W*hen* should he use his gift? To get over on his parents? To change plays like he did in football? To influence his girlfriend? Now seated in his car, Tanner turned the ignition key and sighed. He could get away with practically anything if he wanted to. He backed out of his parking space and headed home; he had a lot of things to think about.

Jeff La Ferney

Chapter 8

Jessie was at Mongolian Barbeque with her friend, Carlee Simpson. It was a noisy restaurant, but a good place to talk anyway, and Carlee liked to talk. Actually, she liked to ask questions and pry into people's personal lives, but she had proven to be a trustworthy friend and someone Jessie was willing to confide in. It was Saturday, one week into the basketball season (that was how the other members of the family kept track of time). The restaurant was hopping, mostly full of happy customers. The entire serving crew just finished singing a birthday song to a middle-aged man at the next table and an aluminum foil swan was placed as a hat on his head...at least it looked like a swan, but maybe it was a sailing ship.

The conversations always started out the same, "So how's the family?"

"It's basketball season, so Tanner's as busy as ever. Clay is different during basketball season. To him, football's just something for Tanner to do, so he doesn't care much about it except to go and watch. But now that it's basketball season, Clay's focused on getting him a good scholarship."

"Any offers?"

"Not really; not yet, but there's interest—mostly from Division 2 schools and some of the smaller Division 1 schools. We get letters and phone calls and Clay takes care of it. We're all doing okay. How's *your* family?"

"We're fine. The girls send about 20,000 texts per month. Drives us both crazy. They carry those stupid phones around with 'em wherever they go. Can't focus on any one thing for a minute straight before the cell vibrates and they read or type another text."

"I know how that is…it's a different world we live in. No task seems as important as the next message. How's the husband?"

"Oh, Mark's started another 'project.' I don't know why he does that. He's the least handy man I know. He was changing some doorknobs a couple days ago and couldn't seem to get one of the old doorknobs off. He ended up using a hacksaw to saw through the stupid thing. By the time he was finished, there were nicks and hacks all over the door. The new doorknob looks decent but the door looks horrible. So I'll have to patch it and paint it myself because he's moved on to a shelving project."

"How's that going?"

"Well," Carlee giggled, "just before I left, I heard a crash and a couple of swear words. The shelf had fallen and he was hopping around on one foot. His big toe was bleeding…quite a bit, actually." She laughed. "He's dangerous with a tool in his hands."

"I remember the toilet story."

"Oh, yeah, a classic. Only Mark can crack a toilet trying to change a toilet seat. I had to call a plumber before he destroyed the whole bathroom." Both women cracked up. Carlee put a forkful of food in her mouth. "I love the food here…so what's *really* up with you, Jessie? Something you want to talk about?" She forked a second helping of grilled vegetables, meats, and sauces into a flour tortilla.

"I don't know. We've talked about this before. Sometimes I just don't really get Clay."

"What do you mean?"

"In certain settings Clay's such a confident guy. But with me, he's so…passive…so weak…so *lacking* in confidence. It seems like I make all the decisions."

"What's wrong with that?" Carlee smiled. "Sounds perfect to me."

"It's *not* perfect. Okay, say I do something that I want to do, and I know *he* doesn't like it. I feel guilty. Heck, I *always* feel guilty."

"For example…?"

"Sometimes it's things I don't even understand, but usually it's things like swimming or eating out or lying in the sun or watching *Desperate Housewives*."

"He doesn't like those things?"

"Nope."

"And you do them anyway?"

"Why shouldn't I? There's nothing wrong with them."

"Even *Desperate Housewives*?"

"Okay, you're missing the point. Let's say I ask him what he'd like to do. So he says that we could go out to eat. I ask him where and he says 'wherever you want.' So we go out to eat, and I *know* he doesn't really want to be there, and I pick the place because it doesn't matter to him…I want him to *want* to go out to eat, and it would be nice if *he* would choose the restaurant."

"Is he unpleasant when you're out?"

"No, but I know he doesn't want to be there, and he's only there because it's what I want. So I end up mad at him."

"Like when you used to buy Christmas trees?"

"Exactly. I knew he didn't want to look for one, pay for one, or set it up in the house. He just did it because it was something I wanted. So regardless how he acted, even if he was being pleasant, I'd always get mad at him. Why couldn't he just *want* to get a Christmas tree? And another thing…" She was getting on a roll now, so Carlee just sat back to listen. "When we disagree about something, why won't he look me in the eyes? I wish he'd just be a man and tell me what to do or what he's thinking."

"Why doesn't he?"

"He says I know how he feels about things. He says we don't have to like the same things. If it isn't morally wrong or if it won't hurt someone else, he says I can choose to do whatever I want. But there's got to be a reason he doesn't look at me. It's like he feels superior and he's looking down on me. Maybe he doesn't really care about me…or maybe he's guilty about something."

"What do *you* think?"

"Well, I think he loves me. He always forgives me, and sometimes I can say some nasty things when I'm mad. I guess I really don't think he somehow feels superior to me either. He tells me how lucky he is to have me. So I can't help but wonder if he's feeling guilty or ashamed about something…except he's always been this way. That's partly why I don't get him."

"What would he be guilty about? Another woman?"

"It's got to be something."

"So is this why you've found a new boyfriend?"

"He's *not* a boyfriend. But he is a friend. And he treats me like I'm special. I like how he treats me."

"And it's not going beyond friendship?"

"Oh, I don't know. Maybe. I don't know. I don't think so, but what would be wrong if it did? It's not like I'm going to leave Clay and Tanner. We have a good family."

"Would you want Clay fooling around?"

"If I wasn't making him happy, I would."

"I've known you for about six years, Jessie, and I *know* you don't mean that. You wouldn't like it one bit."

"Okay, maybe that's true." She hesitated for several seconds. "Do you think I'm wrong, trying to be happy?"

"I always thought you were happy, Jessie. I'm just warning you. You won't even say who the guy is. How can you be sure he won't hurt you?"

"Oh, he would never hurt me—not intentionally."

"Don't be so sure of that." After a few seconds, Carlee said, "Let's box this up and get out of here before I explode. I've got some shoes to show you that I'm thinking about buying…and maybe a purse…and some earrings." The tension was eased as both women began to laugh.

Chapter 9

Jack Harding was in the middle of another unscrupulous gun sale. Jack always had guns to sell, and he just as often had buyers for his guns. Occasionally some clown from the neighborhood would pawn off a gun that he had just stolen. Jack was also in the habit of accepting guns as collateral when setting the terms for one of his predatory loans. He also had a contact from Florida who would once or twice a year bring a trunk load of handguns to sell at a quantity discount. Once in a while, one of Jack's "loan agents" would confiscate a handgun or two from a client who was behind on payments. In any case, if a handgun was needed, Jack was someone to turn to. What he had in his hand at the moment was a Smith and Wesson .38 caliber revolver. The buyer couldn't have been more than 17 years of age, but he had cash, and he had the nerve to show up at Harding Metals earlier in the day and ask the desk clerk if he could speak to the owner. Now at two in the morning, Jack was handing over the revolver and accepting the $350.00 in cash. At that moment, Pete Piggott, who had been summoned to the office, almost certainly to talk about Kevin's playing time, walked through the door and saw the weapon and cash exchanging hands. The teenager, at about 6'4", looked very athletic, but also very angry. His braided hair was long enough to be hanging on his neck. It extended from a flat-billed New York Yankee's cap that was sitting at a crazy angle on his head. He had a tattoo of a chain around his neck. As the kid nervously pocketed the gun, he eyed Piggott with a hateful look that chilled his bones.

Jack assured his customer that no one saw anything. "Get out of here, LaDainian," he ordered. "It was nice doin' business with ya."

The teenager quickly exited while Pete Piggott shook his head in concern. "What do you suppose that kid needed a gun for, Jack? Shootin' cans off the back fence?"

"How the heck would I know? It's no concern of mine."

"Not even if he uses it to kill someone?"

"Gun can't be traced to me. And if I didn't sell it to him, he'd have gotten one some other way. Free enterprise. I'm just capitalizin' on a simple sales opportunity."

".38 Special?"

"Yeah, he wanted a .44 Magnum. Told him that was too much gun for a kid. He didn't like hearin' that from me. Stared me down like he could intimidate me, but I've met angry kids like him before. I just look 'em in the eyes just as cold as they're lookin' at me. Told him I had a .38 or this .22, or he could look somewhere else." He held the gun up for Piggott to see. "He took the Smith and Wesson and paid cash. Probably stole the cash from his mama or grandmama. What's the inner city doin' for kids these days? Hardly any chance at all of growin' up to be a respectable criminal like me." Jack was actually proud of how he turned out. "I wanted to talk to you about basketball, Pete," Jack said as he dropped the .22 in a desk drawer.

"I'm all ears."

"I'm thinkin' you need to be playing Kevin at point guard this year."

"I do that, and he won't be starting."

"And why's that, Pete?"

"Tanner Thomas is my best point guard. Kevin can start at the two guard."

"Tanner Thomas is a punk, and he ain't as good as my Kevin."

"Jack, I don't know much; I'm willing to admit that. Got myself owin' you a fortune, so I'm certain I'm pretty much a dumb twit most of the time, but I do know that Kevin isn't the player that Tanner is. I'm glad to have him; don't get me wrong, but if we expect to win the conference this year, we need to have the ball in Tanner's hands as much as possible."

"And if I tell you to start Kevin at the point, what're you gonna say to that?"

"It'd put me in a bad spot, but I'd like to believe that I'd tell you no. Hopefully, I don't have to do that, Jack. Now, can I get back to work? I'm still repairin' that fence at the back of the property."

"You owe me so much money; I could have one of my goons break your kneecaps."

"You could do that, and I wouldn't like that too much. But do you think my replacement would be wantin' to start your son at the point?"

Pete Piggott was sweating, well, like a pig, as he headed across the junkyard. He was hoping Jack Harding would be more reasonable. Harding's business and criminal enterprise were both growing, and Pete was pretty sure that the only reason he still had a job was because he was coaching Kevin. The criminal industry seemed to be flourishing more. Over the last couple of years, video cameras had been installed for additional security, and one dog had been purchased, though it turned out to be deaf. It'd hide away out of fear of being run over by one of the huge machines in the yard and would only appear when it smelled food. Coach Piggott figured he'd probably lose his job in early March, when the season ended, replaced by more electronic security and several man-eating dogs that could hear. In the meantime, Pete owed Jack thousands of dollars, compounding with exorbitant interest each and every week. He was already making plans to hightail it out of town the moment his team's season ended with a loss in the state tournament. He was thinking of heading toward Windsor, Ontario, where rumor had it Honey Suckle was dancing at one of the clubs. Maybe he could locate her, get married, and hide from Jack Harding the rest of his life.

***

Tanner Thomas had been having a very interesting week. Coach Piggott had been screaming his head off all week and running the players ragged whenever he didn't like their effort or their attitude or the look on their faces or the number on their practice jerseys—whatever came to mind, but luckily not much came to Pete Piggott's mind.

Speaking of minds, Tanner was messing with everyone's. During a huddle after a particularly frustrating drill, Piggott was trying to criticize their stupidity, but was having trouble coming up with the right vocabulary. Kevin Harding happened to look directly at Tanner and was rolling his eyes when Tanner suggested, *"Shoot the ball, Kevin. Shoot it right now."* Inexplicably—a word Coach Piggott would have never thought of—Kevin shot the ball from about 30 feet, hitting nothing but floor and eventually the ball rack, knocking three more balls to the floor.

Coach Piggott, who obviously favored Kevin, could think of nothing to say, but his jaw dropped open and his head fell forward and he finally said, "You stupid, son-of..." but he caught himself before swearing at his boss's son.

Mike Powell, who seemed to like pain and rarely seemed to get tired said, "You need to work on your range a little, Kevin." Then everyone cracked up except the Pigman, who lined the squad up again for a new set of sprints.

Earlier in the day, in third period science, Mr. Henson was demonstrating an experiment. Various students would step inside the giant fifty-plus gallon garbage bags from the custodian's closet. Students would cinch the bag up around their necks, crouch in the bag, and hold the nozzle end of a shop vacuum hose between their legs, making sure the bag was unable to get sucked into the hose. Once the vacuum was turned on, the bag sealed around the student so tightly, he or she would be unable to move. Tanner casually suggested to Mr. Henson, when he got some good eye contact, that he let Tanner and TJ try it together. The crowd of students gathered around with a bit more interest. Both Tanner and TJ squatted in the bag and pulled it around their shoulders. Tanner put the hose nozzle between his legs and Mr. Henson turned on the vacuum. The bag pulled so tightly around the boyfriend and girlfriend that it squeezed them together and they toppled over, TJ

72

directly on top of Tanner. The class erupted into all sorts of hilarious laughter and somewhat inappropriate comments while Henson's face glowed red from embarrassment.

At lunch one day, Tanner got Monica Montegue, who was a ham and might have done it anyway, to sing, "Itsy Bitsy Spider," hand motions and all, to Mr. Jackson, one of the assistant principals. Mr. Jackson was a pretty good guy and he let Monica finish the song.

Just before basketball practice on Friday, Tanner noticed a tiny freshman cheerleader quite thoroughly eyeing Sprout Monroe, one of the team's best players. Tanner told her to give him a kiss. With Sprout being one of the shyest kids—and tallest—in the school, Tanner knew he'd never ask the tiny cheerleader out. The little girl walked up to Sprout then literally jumped up and hung from his shoulders as she kissed him, her feet dangling a foot and a half from the ground. Sprout was smitten with love and Tanner actually felt pretty good about the deed.

It had been a good week. Tanner had some innocent fun, and though he knew he was going to have to eventually sort out appropriate ways to use his newly discovered powers, for the time being, he was having some good-hearted entertainment.

Jeff La Ferney

Chapter 10

Saturday, November 28, was the morning of the preseason scrimmage. It was a four-team affair including Kearsley, a charter school called International Academy of Flint, Flint Hamady, and Flint Beecher. All three were city schools, smaller in size than Kearsley but competitive in basketball. Coach Piggott had been persuaded that beefing up his preseason and non-league schedules would be advantageous once the state tournament began. Piggott was mostly hoping to just get through the year without getting his knee caps broken, but others had higher hopes for the season. Jessie Thomas entered the gym with TJ Harding. Clay was already lagging behind, watching Kearsley and Beecher warming up. He noticed as he approached the coach that Piggott clearly wanted a word with him.

"Mr. Thomas."

"Morning, Coach." Clay thought about offering his hand but decided against that. He was wearing one of his favorite shirts.

"Got Jack Harding puttin' pressure on me to start his son at the point."

"Why're you tellin' me that?"

"Just wanted you to know I told him he could kiss my you-know-what. Gotta let people know who's the boss."

"Wouldn't want you gettin' in trouble with Jack, Coach. I thought you worked for him."

"That's down at the scrap yard. Here in the gym, *I'm* the boss." Pete Piggott's posturing in front of his best player's dad was a defense mechanism—an attempt to make himself feel better about the fact that Jack Harding nearly scared him to death.

"Well, I'm looking forward to a good year, Coach. Have a good scrimmage."

"You too...I mean, enjoy. I guess *you're* not scrimmaging! Ha, that's a good one...'you too!' You didn't bring your shoes, did ya? 'You too.' I'm a stitch!"

Clay finally escaped, grateful to not be touched. He climbed a few rows of bleachers, shook hands with Jack Harding, said hi to a handful of other parents who had already arrived, and sat next to his wife.

"What's Piggott all smiles about, Clay?" Jessie asked. "Don't see him smiling like that too often."

"Seems nervous about something." He leaned close to Jessie so TJ couldn't hear. "I guess Jack's puttin' a little pressure on him to play Kevin at the point. Be interesting to see what happens."

"Do you like that coach, Mr. Thomas?" TJ asked.

"I try to like everybody, TJ. I have to admit that he's a little harder than most to like, but I try."

"Kevin seems to like him for some reason. He seems too sweaty to me," she smiled.

TJ was a sweet girl. Jessie seemed genuinely pleased with Tanner's new girlfriend. Her real name was Tangerine. Tangerine Jacqueleene Harding—her mother had a keen sense of humor. "TJ" fit her nicely though. Cute name; cute girl. She reminded Clay of Jessie. Jessie was the kind of woman he never got tired of looking at. He counted his blessings that she had married him. Clay noticed Tanner looking up at TJ several times during warm-ups. He would smile, then swish another jump shot. His shot looked good. His thigh bruise had pretty much healed, and Clay was looking forward to watching him play again. TJ seemed to be looking forward to it too.

All three opponents during the day attacked with full court pressure. Tanner was handling it nicely, but Coach Piggott kept inserting Kevin into the point guard position and he wasn't doing so well. Piggott would pull him and Jack Harding would start boiling. When Kevin was playing the shooting guard position, he did quite well, but he looked uncomfortable at the point. A junior, up from the JV, by the name of Lance Mankowski, seemed much better suited to backing up Tanner. Kearsley played well, winning the first two scrimmages, but the final one against Hamady was going down to the wire. Hamady was ranked number three in the state in the Class C preseason rankings and was giving Kearsley a great game. At approximately 6'4", their best player, LaDainian Hairston, looked a lot to Coach Piggott like the kid that had bought the gun from Jack Harding—long braided cornrows that ended at a tattooed chain around his neck. And he played angry, reminding the coach of the chill he felt when the kid at Jack's office looked him in the eyes. With 50 seconds to go, Kevin made a turnover and compounded the error with a foul. Coach Piggott pulled him from the game and Jack Harding blew a gasket. While Hamady's star player was making both free throws to take the lead, Harding made his way to the bench. Whatever he said to Piggott was kept quiet enough that no one heard it, but Pete Piggott just about passed out. His body more or less crumpled to the bench, and he began massaging his kneecaps. Tanner noticed the problem and called time out.

"Is there something wrong, Coach?"

Jack Harding made his way out of the gym. Kevin Harding looked mortified and sat with his head in his hands. Piggott was sweating more than usual. "No, everything's fine. Let's see if we can hold the ball for the last shot. It's just a scrimmage. Win or lose, let's just see how we handle this last possession. Thomas, if you get a chance, take it to the hoop and make somethin' happen." That was a lot of words from a man who seemed to be hyperventilating.

Luke Simms inbounded the ball to Tanner. Flint Hamady seemed willing to let the clock wind down, so Tanner dribbled the ball in the backcourt until ten seconds remained. Hamady had dropped back into a 3-2 zone, hoping to keep Kearsley on the perimeter for the last shot. At just under the ten second mark, Tanner passed the ball to his left to Mike Powell, then followed his pass and received a handoff as he ran by. He took two dribbles to the baseline, elevated, and neatly sank a twelve-foot jumper over the outstretched hand of LaDainian Hairston. The horn sounded before Hamady could retrieve the ball from the net. Hairston swore and kicked the ball against the wall. As Kearsley's team celebrated and congratulated Tanner, Coach Piggott and Kevin Harding didn't move from the bench. The crowd, mostly of parents and other family members, managed to clap and cheer a little uncomfortably. The season hadn't even started, yet there was an air of anxiety that was unmistakable. It was going to be an interesting year.

***

The next afternoon, after attending church together, there was almost no discussion in the car. Jessie didn't even ask about eating out, which was very unusual, but Clay was relieved. Everyone, including Clay, seemed preoccupied with his or her own thoughts.

Clay couldn't get the possibility of talking to someone about his mind-control powers out of his mind. From what he had seen and a few things he had heard of late, he was certain that Tanner had discovered that he too could control minds, and he was using the power somewhat recklessly. Clay had been wondering if mind-control powers could be inherited genetically. Could there be a biological reason? Clay was also considering visiting a neurologist because it seemed to be more than a coincidence that both Tanner and he had almost died by strangulation at birth with no side effects. Maybe there was a neurological explanation. Maybe starving the brain of oxygen at birth had influenced each brain in a miraculous way. He was also considering visiting a psychiatrist. It might do him some good to talk out what he'd gone through over the last nearly 30 years. Maybe he could get some insights on how to break the news to his wife and how to guide his son. He dreaded the thought of how Jessie might react, but he actually had hopes that talking to Tanner might improve the relationship that he longed to have with his son. Too often he had stepped aside while his wife had raised his son. Clay was also struggling with what he felt might be horrible consequences if he shared his secret gift with *anyone*, let alone his wife. Deciding what to do was consuming his thoughts.

***

Jessie couldn't get John out of her mind. She wasn't in love with John, but she felt certain that she was falling out of love with Clay. His low self-confidence, his non-assertiveness, and his lack of passion were wearing thin. Was she just going through a mid-life crisis? Was she not justified in expecting more from Clay and wanting more for herself? Was she just being selfish and worldly? What would a split-up do to Tanner and Clay, and how would her parents react? Was John the kind of person she was looking for? Jessie had been warned by Carlee to be careful and to not trust John, but what did Carlee really know about John? Jessie was mildly concerned that she had seen a bit of a temper lately with John, something that she never saw in Clay, but he was still treating her like a queen.

When Jessie was a little girl, she loved the stories of the prince riding in on horseback, rescuing the fair maiden and living with her happily ever after. As beautiful as she was, she somehow always just saw herself as the plain, fair maiden, looking for a fairy tale ending to her life and dreams. When Clay had entered her life, he was so stricken by her that he treated her like the princess she had always dreamed she'd be. She fell in love with him because he had loved her so much. When she first became pregnant with Tanner, she had visions of a large, perfect, happy family, but then she almost lost her only child and she was unable to have others. Her dreams would never be completely fulfilled. She remembered very little about that day. She recalled Clay telling her that it wasn't her fault, and she believed him, but she didn't know *why* she might have believed it was her fault. Her lack of memory of that day had nagged her over the years, but currently those thoughts were overpowered by what she was going to do next about John.

***

Tanner could hardly concentrate now that he understood his power. He'd decided to keep it a secret, but he was using it so much that he felt that he was losing control of it. He wasn't afraid

79

it wouldn't work; rather, he was afraid that he was going to hurt someone or lose who he really was. He was having a blast, almost addictively playing with his power, but he wanted a scholarship that he earned and a girlfriend that liked him for who he was. He feared disappointing his parents or slipping up and being discovered and losing those who were close to him. The debate was simple: use the power for his own benefit or not? The conclusion thus far had been to use it.

Chapter 11

Pete Piggott was on edge and barely slept the rest of the weekend. It was now third shift on Sunday night and Pete was tired—tired and scared. What was he going to do about Jack Harding? He couldn't quit his job; he owed Jack too much money. He couldn't be looking over his shoulder every minute of the day either; the season was too long for that. If he valued his kneecaps, and he rather did value them, was he going to have to give Kevin the point guard job? The last thing Jack had said before storming out of the gym was, "I wasn't kidding when I said I could have your kneecaps broken." Pete needed some protection.

Usually on Sundays, Pete arrived at the salvage yard ahead of Jack. He would go into the office, punch in his time card, and start a pot of bad coffee. It was cold at night in late November, so Pete wouldn't leave the office until he had to, and he wouldn't leave without a tall cup of coffee. On this particular night, however, Pete had something additional in mind. Jack Harding had dropped that .22 in a drawer in his desk. If Pete needed protection, a gun might do the trick. He carefully opened the drawer, and sure enough, the gun was there.

It was a Ruger .22 caliber pistol. With only a four and a half inch barrel, it could easily be hidden in the pocket of his coat. The precision-molded polymer grip included an internal safety lock and a ten-round magazine. Pete was pretty certain he was more likely to shoot himself than any goons trying to break his kneecaps, but he felt safer with the gun in his pocket anyway. With his coat buttoned, hat pulled over his ears, gloves in place, and large coffee cup in hand, Pete left the office and started his first trip around the salvage yard. When he returned, intent on refilling his coffee cup, Jack was seated in his desk chair, waiting.

"Have a seat, Pete." Piggott dropped into the chair and unbuttoned his coat so he didn't look quite so much like an abominable snowman. "I guess it's time I made a few things clear to you. You owe me money, and it's time to pay up."

"You know I can't pay you, Jack. I already give you a third of my check, but each week the balance is bigger than the week before."

"That's true; so what do you propose we do about that?"

"I already paid back better'n ten times what I've borrowed over the years. How 'bout forgiving the debt."

"How 'bout you play Kevin at the point and I hold off breaking your kneecaps?"

"First game's Tuesday. That's what you want? Kevin plays the point instead of Thomas?"

"That'll keep your knees healthy for a couple more days. And if I tell you to take the Thomas kid out, take him out."

"Out of the game?" Afraid for his own well-being, Piggott realized that his boss had him backed into a corner. "Okay, Jack, I can see you're serious. Whatever you say. Now I got some work to do." Pete leaned back and then thrust his head forward over his belly, propelling himself with difficulty from his chair. As his fat body lunged forward, his coat swung backward and the handle of his .22 banged against the arm of the chair. Pete sucked in a quick breath and tried as best as he could to glance casually at Jack. Jack didn't seem to notice, however; he was smiling and already looking forward to Tuesday.

***

On Tuesday night, a decent crowd showed up for the Kearsley Hornets' home opener. It was a league game against Lapeer West. The West JV team won by a dozen points, but Kearsley's varsity was the favorite in the nightcap. Clay was sitting about four feet from Jessie.

82

On the way out of the house, Jessie couldn't find her purse. As she raced around the house, Clay was petting the dog. "Aren't you going to *help*?"

"Do you *need* your purse? You'll more'n likely leave it in the car once we get to the game."

"Of course I need my purse. I *always* take my purse."

"And then you leave it in the car once we get to the game."

"There are things that I need."

"What good are they if you leave your purse in the car?"

"Then I won't leave it in the car, okay!"

"Did you check by the door?"

Jessie rolled her eyes, then checked by the door. There it was. She walked back into the kitchen and began to cry. Clay attempted to put his arms around her, but she pushed him away. "If you would have helped, I wouldn't be so frazzled. If you knew it was by the door, why didn't you go get it?"

"I didn't know it was by the door. It was just a suggestion. Come on; let's go to the game. You're just nervous about the game tonight. I'm nervous too. Tanner's gonna do great."

"I needed my chap stick; that's why I needed my purse. You could have helped."

Once in the parking lot at the game, when exiting the vehicle, Jessie left her purse on the passenger side floor. Clay restrained from saying something. It was that time of the month, obviously, and that meant to be careful. So Clay was giving Jessie a little room in the bleachers. Jessie was glad for the room. She didn't want Clay close to her. If he cared more about her, he would have helped her find her purse. John was more considerate than Clay. Plus John would be in the crowd and she didn't want Clay practically in her lap. The room was just what she needed. The horn sounded, calling an end to pre-game warm-ups, and the crowd rose for the playing of the National Anthem. Lapeer West's starters were announced and then the lights went down and a spotlight illuminated Kearsley's bench. The spotlight would be aimed at each starter as he ran to half court.

The public address announcer began with Mike Powell at one forward. Mike was about 6'2", 210 pounds. He wasn't a great basketball player, but he was strong and physical like the football player that he was. He played tough defense and rebounded very well, but he didn't score much.

The next forward announced, at about 6'3", was Luke Simms. Luke ran the floor well and, ironically, was on the receiving end of a lot of Tanner Thomas passes, the opposite of the football season. He had been a sophomore on the team last year and started the last few games.

The starting center, Tommy "Sprout" Monroe, was called next. Last year before Christmas break, Tommy was a 5'11" backup guard who needed work on his ball handling. One week later, he showed up at practice at 6'4." He literally "sprouted" five inches. He miraculously "blossomed" from a guard with forward skills to a forward with guard skills, which happened to be a much better package. Luke Simms had looked Tommy over carefully and asked, "Hey, Sprout, did it hurt?" which was a question everyone was wondering. The nickname stuck, and after two additional inches of growth, Tommy was now the 6'6" center for a very good team. He was a third-team all-leaguer last year.

Kevin Harding was announced as one starting guard. He was 5'11" and had a pretty nice shooting stroke. He wasn't very comfortable running the show, but handled the ball reasonable well as a secondary ball handler. He made all-conference honorable mention as a junior.

The star of the team was announced last, Tanner Thomas. Tanner was a 6'2", 188 pound point guard with great handles, terrific speed, and a silky-smooth jump shot. He averaged over 17 points per game as a junior and was getting some attention from Division 1 colleges. This was his team, and Tanner was the kind a leader who was poised, confident, and exciting to watch. There was a great cheer in the crowd as his name was announced as the fifth starter. Clay looked at Jessie, who was crying again and obviously looking for her purse, forgetting that she had left it in the car—tissues, make-up, chap stick, and all.

In the huddle, just before tip-off, Coach Piggott made his announcement. "Harding, you're at the point. Thomas, you move to two. Simms, you're three; Powell, you're four; Sprout, you're five. We're in man defense; pick 'em up as soon as you'd like. Remember, they like to pound it inside, but keep your eye on number 22; he's a pretty good shooter. Any questions?"

"Yeah," Kevin said. "Why am I at the point?"

"Because I said so! If you have a problem with that, let me know right now. There's prob'ly an empty seat for you down near the end of the bench. Now let's go!"

On the way to the opening tip, Kevin asked Tanner if he was going to take the point anyway.

"No. Just do what he says."

Sprout won the opening tap. Luke Simms tossed it to Harding and the game began…with a Harding turnover that led to a Lapeer West basket. Clay glanced over at Jack Harding while wondering what was going on. West pressured the inbounds pass, but Simms managed to get the ball to Tanner, who broke the pressure easily. As he pushed the ball up the court, the Lapeer defender backpedaled into the lane, and Tanner pulled up and nailed a three-pointer to get the Hornets on the board. Kevin pressured the Lapeer ball handler up the court. The guard tried a pass to the wing that Tanner intercepted and took the length of the court, finishing with a dunk and drawing a foul. Tanner made the free throw for a 6-2 lead, and Lapeer West's coach called a quick time out.

Piggott was actually smiling when he turned and saw Jack Harding mouth, plain as day, "Take… him…out." Coach's face turned red, his sweat glands opened, and he told Lance Mankowski to check in for Tanner Thomas. Tanner didn't play another minute for the rest of the half. Kevin Harding played the point. He handled and shot the ball poorly, and Lapeer West was ahead 37-19 at half time. Jessie was fit to be tied, yelling at Coach Piggott, crying again, then somehow blaming Clay for the benching. Clay sat on the bleachers, staring angrily at Pete Piggott and wondering what in the world to do. Jack Harding wasn't too pleased with his son's play, but he blamed Kevin's teammates and smirked at Clay Thomas. He thought Clay's face was priceless.

In the locker room, Tanner was so upset that he was staring arrows at the Pigman. But Coach Piggott would have nothing to do with Tanner. He never looked at him once. Whenever someone tried to question why Tanner wasn't playing, Piggott told him to shut up. The entire team reentered the gym without a hint of enthusiasm. Kevin Harding had eight turnovers and was one-for-seven from the floor for two points. Clay could see Tanner trying to get Coach Piggott's attention, but he simply wouldn't look at Tanner, and Tanner was practically chasing him in a circle to get the Pigman to look him in the eyes. Clay was more certain than ever, as he watched Tanner in fascination, that Tanner had the "power." It was going to be interesting to see what happened the rest of the game.

Simms, Powell, Monroe, Harding, and Mankowski started the second half. As the ball was inbounded, Coach Piggott lifted a water bottle to his lips, and his eyes settled on Tanner Thomas's. Immediately he said, "Thomas, you're in for Harding." The fat man sat, wondering what he was thinking and why he had put Tanner back in the game. He was sure he was about to have a heart attack. The next half an hour was a nightmare for the Pigman. Four times, when he got his breathing under control, he told Harding to go into the game for Thomas, and each time before Thomas could even sit down, he decided to tell Thomas to go back in for Harding, and each time Tanner entered the game, he was spectacular. Finally Piggott gave up, and finally Jack Harding left the gym, looking like he could kill Pete Piggott, and finally the Kearsley Hornets took the lead. Tanner had 29 second-half points and willed his team to victory.

Chapter 12

Clay knew that it was time to speak to Tanner. When his son got home from practice on Wednesday evening, Clay suggested that they go out for a hamburger and have a talk. Tanner saw that his father was serious and began to make an excuse for not going. Some of the developments in Tanner's life of late had been weighing on him and talking to his dad wasn't what he wanted to do at the moment. Serious talks with his dad were not a very common occurrence, and Tanner wanted to keep it that way.

"I can't, Dad…"

"Yes, you can, and you will." Clay's eyes were locked on Tanner's. This was the first time he was sure he had used his power on his son since Tanner was seven years old and Clay had told him he hated the rain.

"Okay, Dad. Let me put my stuff in my room."

They went to a Coney Island, which had booths and some privacy, something that Clay felt was important for this particular discussion.

"We haven't talked about the game last night. What happened?"

"I don't know. It was like Pig, I mean Piggott, was scared about somethin'. He never said a word, 'cept 'shut up' when someone tried to reason with him."

"Did *you* try to 'reason' with him?" Clay made those little quotation marks with the first two fingers of each hand.

"He wouldn't talk to me…wouldn't even look at me. I tried to talk to him at halftime."

"Yeah, I saw. It was pretty comical, actually, how he kept turning his back on you, and you were chasing him around in a circle."

"Frustrating is a better word. I just wanted him to look me in the eyes, but he wouldn't do it."

"How'd you get him to look at you?"

"Chance…luck."

"So you told him to put you in?"

"No," Tanner sort of lied—he hadn't actually *said* anything. "But he did decide to put me in."

"You didn't have anything to do with that?"

Tanner was getting very uncomfortable. This was something he had decided that he wasn't going to tell anyone about, but he didn't like lying to his dad. "I didn't say anything to him. He just decided to put me in."

Clay sighed a deep sigh. Tanner had a bad feeling about this. He was about to tell his father that they didn't want to have this conversation. He would make his father give up the topic. But something strange happened. In his head he heard, "*I have the same power you do.*"

In *his* head, Clay heard, "*Did you just tell me you have the same power I do?*"

Without speaking, Clay replied, "*Yes, I did. And it's time we talked about it.*"

"Dad, you can alter people's minds?"

"I can make them think what I want them to think, just like you can."

"How is it possible? And how did you know? Can you *read* my mind?"

"No, I can't read minds…just influence them. I don't know how it's possible. I think something happened in our brains when we were born. I know you're doing it because I've watched you."

"I just figured this out in the last couple of months. I figured it was something I should never tell anyone about."

Clay fought back the urge to cry. For the first time in his life, there was someone who might just understand what he'd gone through the past 30 years. "I reached the same conclusion years and years ago." Clay swallowed hard and took a deep breath. He was talking about his powers for the first time in his life, and he was doing it with his son, someone with whom his relationship had certainly suffered because of Clay's silence. "Once, when I was 12 or 13, I was pitching in a baseball game. I'd look the batters in the eyes and think, 'You know you can't hit me.' It was weird because they'd get this look, like they were really uncomfortable up there. I could see in their eyes that they didn't believe they could hit me. Now, I was pretty good—threw pretty hard and had my share of success—but this was like some sort of new mind game. I'd tell the batter to swing and then throw something horrible, out of the strike zone, and they'd swing. I'd tell them I was throwing a fastball and then I'd throw a curve and they'd bail out, looking like an idiot. I'd tell them to take a pitch and then throw one right down the middle and they wouldn't swing. After I threw two no hitters in a row, I began to feel guilty. The next time I pitched, I decided to not use the mind games. Funny, but I gave up a couple of hits and all of a sudden, I didn't think I could get anyone out. I was getting shelled when it started raining. It was one of the only times in my life that I was glad it was raining."

"So you stopped using your powers?"

"Not completely. I had a few lessons to learn still, but I didn't use them too often. I didn't like how I felt when I did it. Guilt. Shame. I wanted to know that what I'd accomplished was because I deserved it; I'd earned it somehow. Let me give you another example. There was this girl when I was in tenth grade. She was beautiful, the catch of the school, but she never acted like she even knew who I was. I thought I'd be happy if she was my girlfriend, so I told her to like me. And she did. For a couple of days, it was awesome. I was cool; I had the hottest girlfriend in the school. But it didn't take long before I didn't like it at all. She'd follow me around, call me on the phone, write me love notes. She was always touching me. Not only was I suffocating, but I also knew she only liked me because I told her to. It didn't give me any pleasure knowing I'd made her like me. She didn't have a choice. It would have been much better if she had decided to like me on her own. Does that make sense to you?"

"Dad, I told Coach Piggott to put me in the game—about four times actually. He kept taking me out, and I kept makin' him put me back in."

"I know. I watched you do it."

"Was I wrong? I actually don't feel very good about it, but I should have been in the game, and we were losing."

"Something's going on with your coach and Mr. Harding. I'm sure of it. I don't blame you for anything, Tanner. If I were you, I'd have probably done the same thing. But this 'gift' we have, I think of it as more of a curse."

"What do you mean?"

Clay paused, trying to sort his thoughts further. "The Apostle Paul wrote in the Bible about how God had given him a 'thorn in the flesh.' Some people think it was bad eyesight or some physical deformity or other health problem, but that's not what I think. Paul wrote that he had spent three years with Jesus and was actually taken up into Heaven. He called Heaven 'paradise', and he wrote that he heard and saw 'inexpressible things' that he wasn't permitted to tell to others. He said God gave him a thorn in the flesh to keep him from becoming conceited. He wrote that the thorn in the flesh 'tormented' him, and he asked God to take it away, but God wouldn't. When I really thought about that, I began to look at my power as a gift, sort of like God showing Heaven to Paul. But then he was told that he couldn't share what he knew with anyone else. When God made Paul keep it to himself, the knowledge tormented the man in some way. I've often thought that maybe God gave me a gift too, but instead of being able to use it and talk about it, it torments me each and every day. The gift itself might be a blessing, but keeping it to myself or using it has been a curse."

"And using it, like to pitch a no-hitter or to get a girlfriend," Tanner interjected, "makes you conceited or you feel terrible about it."

"Exactly. One or the other. I think you understand."

"So you think I shouldn't have made Piggott put me in the game?"

"No, I don't actually believe that. You didn't take away Piggott's choice because I think Mr. Harding took it away first. If Piggott had his first choice, he would've been playing you. And I don't think you were actually being selfish, like you wanted to play so you could score points and get headlines. I think you were thinking of the team. But there'll be consequences; I'm pretty sure of that. Harding has a screw loose and Piggott's stuck in the middle of all of this. Something bad is gonna happen."

"What should I do, Dad?"

"We all have our own consciences to deal with, Tanner. It's not my place to decide for you. In some ways, Son, I haven't felt like a good dad to you because I've let you make your own choices. I've backed off and let your mother train you up because I wanted you to decide for yourself. I wanted to be confident knowing that the choices you made were *yours* instead of mine. I would like it, though, when you make your future choices that you would try to do what's right."

"Do you always know what to do?"

"Not always, Tanner; not always."

Jeff La Ferney

Chapter 13

Jack Harding hadn't showed up at Harding Metals on Tuesday night and Pete had managed to avoid him on Wednesday, but when Pete showed up for work on Thursday after practice, there Jack was, waiting. He was sitting on the edge of his desk, holding a sawed-off shotgun. Pete flinched noticeably, and Jack began laughing. "I ain't plannin' on shootin' ya, Pete—not yet anyway. Some gangbanger from the neighborhood just pawned this off to me a coupla minutes ago. Needed some cash to help out his sister who got herself in some trouble. I'll shoot ya some other time, Pete. Now, tell me what happened the other night."

"Can't tell ya, 'cept for I think I had a heart attack. Somewhere between hyperventilations, I kept telling Thomas to go into the game. Then I'd panic, thinkin' about you, and I'd take 'im out. But then I'd change my mind again and put 'im back in."

"That's a lot of thinkin' for you, all in one night."

Piggott shrugged. There was nothing to say.

"Have to admit, I was pretty perturbed, but then I got to thinkin'. Pete Piggott stood up to me, and that takes guts. I don't like it, but I got to admit, I'm surprised enough by it to give you another chance."

"Jack, Kevin had a terrible game. Don't you think he's smart enough to know it was you who put me up to playin' him at the point instead of Thomas? And you who had me bench Tanner? He's an above average shooting guard and a below average point guard. Can't you see that?"

"What I can see is that Tanner Thomas takes the attention away from my kid. What'd he have, 40 points?"

Piggott shrugged again, though he knew it was 35.

"I've got a proposition for you, Coach. I owe one of my business associates—you know him, name's Johnny Papalli—'bout four grand for a delivery here a week or so ago. Says he attends a lotta games and seems to have taken a real liking to your boy, Thomas. Wanted to bet me two large that Thomas gets at least 20 tomorrow night, and another two grand that Kearsley wins by at least ten points. So I got to thinkin' real fast like a man of my intellect does every so often, that who but you can better control those two outcomes, savin' me several thousand dollars? So here's my proposition: Make sure Thomas gets less than 20, and make sure your team wins by less than ten. You do that and I'll subtract four grand from what you owe me. I'm thinking that maybe now you'll be a little better motivated. So what do ya think?" Jack repositioned the shotgun across his lap, so that both barrels were aimed at Piggott's protruding belly.

Piggott didn't have to think too long about it this time. He agreed to the proposition right away.

***

Harding Metals was a large scrap yard—45 acres of scrapped autos and other waste metal. The property included a 4,000 square foot storage facility/garage. Stacked inside, according to government specifications, were layers and layers of used tires, which were occasionally sold to needy customers. It was in that storage facility that machines for discarded batteries and waste containers for motor oil, gasoline, anti-freeze, mercury switches, and freon were stored, all carefully within government guidelines. Harding made more money with his criminal interests, but he couldn't afford to be shut down by not obeying governmental waste standards. A ten-foot high chain link fence, topped by two rows of barbed wire, surrounded the scrap yard. At each corner of the lot, there was an outbuilding, either a shed or a trailer. Each had electricity, heat, a coffee pot, and a mini-fridge that was kept stocked with drinks. At each building and at the two large gates, there were security cameras and motion activated floodlights. As Piggott walked around the yard, the floodlights would light his way. In addition to the original purchase, Jack had collected quite a bit of heavy machinery for his metal yard, including a 7,000 pound lift, two welders, a front end loader, two tow trucks, a 3,000 pound Yale forklift, a 12,000 pound Hasco forklift, a dump truck, a 42 foot Transcraft flatbed, a Big Mac car crusher, various shipping containers, and a waste-oil furnace.

In addition to the machinery and the outbuildings, there were always junked cars, tractors, campers, and mobile homes, so there were always lots of places to sit down and think, lots of places to ponder how his life had turned out. Pete sat on the seat of a Massey Ferguson lawn tractor which had caught fire and been totaled. At least the seat wasn't a charred mess. He knew that if he could have just kept his temper when that stupid, irritating paperboy was harassing him, he'd have never met Jack Harding. But then he probably would have never become a coach either, and the only things in his lifetime for which he was proud were his high school basketball career and his high school coaching career. And though he admittedly was less than spectacular at even those two things, at least he wasn't a loser. Eight seasons and he only had one losing record. He'd won two league championships and one district championship and felt confident he'd add to both totals this year. But now Jack Harding was asking him to shave points in a basketball game, destroying any pride he had in his career, and Pete was going to let it happen. He was about to become a loser at everything.

***

Game number two was at Swartz Creek High School in a tiny gym that held only about 800 fans. It was the Dragons first home game and their best player, Robbie Dixon, was a preseason all-league pick, who was also a teammate of Tanner Thomas's on their AAU team. There was a good crowd that included TV cameras from ABC Channel 12, and a live blog going out from M-Live, a local on-line newspaper. Clay Thomas was asked to keep the Kearsley scorebook because the regular scorekeeper was home with the flu, so he was seated at the scorer's table at half-court between the two benches. Jack Harding found a seat in the uppermost corner of the bleachers in the balcony. He didn't want anyone accusing him of any underhanded influence on the game. He was confident of winning his 4,000 dollar wager within the next 90 minutes or so.

It appeared that Kearsley had the better team, but the score was close at half-time. Tanner Thomas sat about six minutes, but Lance Mankowski was playing adequately as his backup, and Kevin Harding had nine points at the half. Thomas made eight straight free throws in the second quarter and had 13 points. The score was 38-34 in favor of Kearsley. The score was looking good to Pete Piggott, but the concern was how to not lose the game and keep Tanner Thomas to six points or less. In the locker room, the Pigman announced that he wanted his team to slow the ball down. The strategy seemed odd, since Robbie Dixon was in foul trouble with three, and common sense would suggest that they speed up the game, making Dixon play defense as many possessions as possible in hopes of fouling him out. His 16 points were keeping the Dragons in the game.

The pace of the game turned to a crawl in the second half. Piggott asked his players to slow the game down, and Swartz Creek went into a 2-3 zone to protect Dixon. The Hornets were playing right into the hands of the Dragon team. Three minutes elapsed before Tanner hit a jumper for the first points of the third quarter. The score was 40-34, a six point lead, and Thomas had 15 points, both numbers making Coach Piggott uncomfortable, so Thomas was pulled from the game. When Thomas came out, so did Dixon, and both players remained on the bench throughout the rest of the quarter. The score was 44-39 at the end of three.

Dixon reentered the game to start the fourth, but with three fouls, he was no longer in serious foul trouble. Tanner Thomas remained on the bench. Tanner had determined that he was not going to interfere with Piggott's decisions in this game, for better or for worse, but he was steaming when at the three minute mark of the final quarter, Swartz Creek took the lead, 51-50. Piggott called a time out. Clay Thomas found himself smack dab in the middle of a moral dilemma. He was certain by now that Tanner had decided to stay out of Piggott's mind, but when Piggott looked to the scorer's table and asked Clay how many time outs he had left, Clay said, "Two," and he thought, *"Put Tanner in right now!"* Piggott immediately broke eye-contact with Mr. Thomas and told Tanner to check in the game.

Tanner had an intensity that only the special ones have. He took the inbounds pass, dribbled to about six feet from the three-point line and let loose a shot that hung in the air nearly four seconds before settling perfectly into the bottom of the net. Thomas now had 18 points and Kearsley had the lead by two. Piggott sent Lance Mankowski to the scorer's table to replace Tanner. Swartz Creek's coach asked at the scorer's table how many timeouts *he* had left, but Clay Thomas caught his eyes and very plainly thought, *"Do* not *call a timeout." He* did not want the clock to stop so that Mankowski could get into the game. Without calling a time-out, the Dragons took their time and finally worked the ball into Robbie Dixon's hands, but his shot banged off the back of the rim and into the hands of Sprout Monroe. Monroe fed Thomas, who pushed the ball the length of the floor, and double-pumped a left-handed lay-up between two defenders. It was good, plus Dixon committed his fourth foul. Tanner made the free throw, a Swartz Creek player called a time-out, and Lance Mankowski officially was checked into the game. Thomas had 21 points.

Swartz Creek missed their field goal attempt once play resumed, and Monroe again got the rebound. A Dragon defender fouled immediately to stop the clock. Their five-point deficit turned to seven; and their seven-point deficit turned to eight with another made free throw after a Dragon turnover. Dixon lofted a three-pointer with seconds remaining and the missed shot landed in Kevin Harding's hands. In an act of futility, Kevin was fouled with 2.6 seconds on the clock, and he calmly sank both free throws, giving the Hornets a ten-point victory. Kevin Harding had just cost his dad and his coach 2,000 dollars. Tanner Thomas had cost both men an additional 2,000 dollars. Kevin, Tanner, and Clay had no idea what was going on. Pete Piggott looked like he had seen a ghost. Jack Harding sat in the far corner of the bleachers way up in the balcony, trying to determine what he was going to do next.

Chapter 14

After the game, Coach Piggott never said a word to his team. He looked to his players like he was going to be sick, so everyone assumed that he simply wasn't feeling well. Piggott knew better. He'd just lost himself 4,000 dollars, and worse yet, he'd lost it for Jack Harding as well. There was no way to explain what had just happened. Pete was mentally calculating how much money he had if he were to pick up and run while his knees were still able to function, and what was making him ill was the knowledge that he had nothing. He didn't have enough to spend the night somewhere along his flight route. He was thinking of the .22 he'd been carrying around at work each night and wondering if he had the courage to use it. The team seemed conscious that something was wrong but not overly concerned about what it was, and Pete was relieved that they weren't waiting for any pearls of wisdom. Wisdom and Piggott were not synonymous.

***

Jack Harding's phone rang while he was still sitting in the stands simmering. "Hey, Johnny P. You callin' to gloat?"

"Tell you what, Jack, it sure looked to me like that that coach of yours was doing his best to make sure I didn't win that bet."

"Piggott's best is never good enough," Jack thought. "That Piggott's got to be the dumbest coach I ever seen, Johnny. There's no tellin' why or what that man's doin'. He actually thinks Tanner Thomas is better than my son."

"Your boy had himself a pretty darn good game tonight, Jack, but even a fool like Piggott can see that Thomas is the best player on that team. I hate to break that to ya, but it's the truth."

"If he'd put Kevin at the point, you'd see how good he is."

"Seems like I saw him there last game and he didn't do so hot. He's not a bad player at the wing though. Had double figures tonight, but he didn't have 21 like Thomas. Cha Ching!" Johnny couldn't resist the temptation to be a bad sport.

"I'm sick of that Clay Thomas gettin' everything he wants."

"Don't know what that has to do with anything, but I'll tell you what. I'll get back with ya before the next game and give you a chance to win your four grand back. Even if I lose, I'll still get what ya owe me originally, and I've had a little fun with ya in the meantime."

"It's a deal, Papalli. Talk to ya soon." Jack ended the call and thought to himself, *"Next time, I'll make* sure *I win. I'll remove Piggott from the picture if I have to, and then that idiot can't mess things up."* As Jack pondered what to do, he began wondering how to eliminate Tanner from the picture instead. Getting his money back was a point of pride for Jack Harding, but hurting Clay Thomas was becoming his goal in life. How could he do both next time?

***

Tanner Thomas couldn't understand why he was spending so much time on the bench, and he wondered if his dad was right about Jack Harding having something to do with it. As he reviewed the game, however, he felt good about the fact that he hadn't used his powers to interfere. They had won the game, and that was what mattered most. But as Tanner entered the house when he arrived home, it didn't take more than one look at his father, sitting alone in the kitchen, to realize that his *dad* had done something to interfere.

"At the end of the game, I made Piggott put you in, and I wouldn't let the other coach call a timeout. It got you only an extra minute or so of playing time, but you put the game away. I'm sorry I did it though."

100

"Forget about it, Dad."

Just then Jessie entered the kitchen. She started right in with Tanner. "I don't know what's wrong with that coach of yours, but he's keeping you out of the games on purpose. What does he think he's doing?"

"I don't know, Jess," Clay remarked. "In my opinion, it has something to do with Jack Harding. I think Jack's somehow responsible."

"Don't be ridiculous! He wasn't down there on the bench making decisions. As a matter-of-fact, I didn't see him anywhere around tonight. It's Piggott that must have something against you, Tanner."

"Pete told me that Jack was pressuring him. Remember? Piggott's a weasel. He'd do whatever Jack told him to."

"Mr. Harding's just a parent, just like you and me. It's the *coach* that's cheating our son. How could you accuse Jack Harding?" And Jessie walked away.

Both Tanner and Clay watched her storm down the hall and into her bedroom. Clay shrugged his shoulders and let her go without another word.

"TJ seems to think that her dad has something against *you*, not me, Dad. She says he gets mad every time he hears your name."

"Well, if that's true, I don't understand it. I've never had one problem, one conflict with Jack. I can't see why he'd have anything against me. Now you, *you* are getting attention that he wants for Kevin. I can see what he might have against you. What I *don't* see, if your mother is right, is what Coach Piggott would have against you."

***

Piggott tried to slither into work unnoticed that Friday night after the game. For a man built like a bowling ball, sneaking around was not an easy thing to accomplish. He might be able to hide behind one of the front-end loaders without his belly protruding, but sneaking around the office door to get his time card punched would be next to impossible, especially since a meeting with Jack and his brood of hoodlums was going on in the office.

Pete fingered the pistol in his coat pocket, said a quick prayer to whatever god might be listening, and entered the office.

"What are you doing here, Pete?" Jack asked, dark eyes glaring more darkly than usual.

"Um, I was going to punch in and then do my job."

"You're not too good at 'doing your job,' Coach. Thought maybe money would be a good incentive for you, but I guess not." Piggott just kept his eyes on the floor and his hand on his gun grip. "Is there anything you *are* good at, Pete, besides being a fool, I mean."

After quite an unpleasant two or three seconds of silence, Pete Piggott finally looked up and said, "I'm not too bad at coaching basketball, Jack. And I especially think I'm not doing too bad a job of coachin' your son."

"Get out, Pete. I'm giving you a one-week leave of absence. Paid leave. I got some business to do, and I don't want you around for a while. Come back for work next Friday, and your check'll be waiting."

Piggott turned and walked out. As far as he could figure, something he wasn't known to do too often, there was nothing wrong with not having to work, getting paid, and not having to be around Jack Harding for a while. Piggott was already making plans for the strip clubs. *"I wonder if Honey Suckle is back in town."*

***

As soon as Piggott had exited, Jack and his goons went back to their meeting. Jack was making plans, real plans this time, to humiliate Clay Thomas, get his money back, and get his son, Kevin, the attention that he deserved. If Jack Harding was anything, he was resourceful. Give him a challenge, and he would use every resource possible to meet it, even if it meant breaking the law. With the possible exception of money, and occasionally his family, nothing was more important to Jack than his pride. Clay Thomas would be taken down a notch, and that meant that whatever was important to Clay was to become a target for Jack.

Chapter 15

Carlee Simpson was concerned. She had known Jessie Thomas for six years. They had become fast and best friends almost from the time Jessie, Clay, and Tanner had moved to Flint. In those six years, she had admired Jessie Thomas's positive outlook on life and her spirit for living. Sure, she could be emotional at times, but it was part of the package that included a zest for living. Carlee had cheated one time on her husband about three years ago and had shared her mistake with Jessie, so Jessie felt comfortable sharing her experiences with Carlee. The stories about Tony, the resident at the clinic, seemed harmless, and nothing had come of it, but the stories about this newest man were disturbing to Carlee, mostly because Jessie was keeping secrets and getting serious and partly because Jessie had shared that she'd seen a hint of a bad temper lately. Carlee warned Jessie that assuredly, this man would be on his best behavior at this point in the relationship. If there were signs of temper now, there was almost certain to be a worse temper to be discovered.

Carlee remembered some scary times with her father while she was growing up. Once in a fit of road rage, he had literally smashed a car on the expressway that supposedly had cut him off. The driver swerved off the road, through a ditch, and directly under a billboard that ironically said, "Buckle Up for Safety." Another time, when her family was bumped from an airplane flight, her father put up such a fit that he was eventually handcuffed and placed in a holding cell. The family took the next flight while her father was detained. Carlee never heard what happened to her father, but she remembered how embarrassed her mother was. One morning, her father shoved her mother to the floor because of an argument that his egg yolks were overcooked. That same day, while her father was away at work, the whole family moved out of the house and into her grandparents' home. When Carlee heard the word *temper*, it raised red flags that she was unwilling to ignore. She decided to call and ask for help, and the one person who came to her mind first was her cousin, a Mr. Pete Piggott, head security guard at Harding Metals.

Carlee was the only family that Pete Piggott had. They weren't close. Who would want to be close to Pete Piggott? But she had a soft spot for him because he was family and he seemed so helpless and hopeless most of the time. What appealed to her in this particular circumstance was that Pete had security background, and because he worked third-shift at Harding Metals, he would likely be available for a little sleuthing. She could hire him, knowing he needed money. He always needed money. Carlee called her cousin, Pete, and set up a meeting.

***

"I need a favor."

Pete had just entered Carlee's home. Angela and Heather were sitting on the couch, texting. Angela had the TV remote, and between texts, Heather was asking for it. Angela was somehow channel surfing, texting, and doing her homework. It was unlikely that she heard her sister with her IPod playing in her ears. Neither even looked up when their mother's cousin entered the room.

Mark had a cordless screwdriver in one hand and a roll of electrical tape in the other. He said, "Hey, Pete," as he scooted down the stairs to either continue a project or make repairs on one of his inevitable disasters, one or the other.

"Have a seat, Pete. It's good to see you."

Piggott took off his jacket and grabbed a chair by the dining room table—he would never have felt comfortable sitting in the living room near Carlee's girls. When he sat his short, fat frame in his chosen dining room chair, Carlee burst out laughing. Mark had just "repaired" the chair before heading to the basement for his next project. The chair legs had worn unevenly, so the chair wobbled and bumped from one leg to another whenever someone shifted weight in it. Mark's goal was to shorten the other legs slightly to match the worn one. He measured and then cut, and then cut, and then cut. Now the chair that Pete Piggott was sitting in had to be nearly three inches shorter than the rest of the chairs, and the table nearly came to Piggott's neck. At least it wasn't wobbling.

Carlee sat in a different chair and towered over her cousin as she attempted to make some small talk. Realizing that the girls shouldn't be privy to her requested favor, she sent them to their rooms. A drilling sound was coming from the basement, so Carlee felt she only had a few minutes before the next emergency. She cut the small talk short, once the girls were gone, and got right to the point.

"I need you to follow someone for me."

"Like detective work?"

"Yeah, you're a security man. Surely you know a little about staking someone out?"

"Oh, yeah. Of course. It's all part of the job description." Pete Piggott had no idea about "staking someone out."

"Well, I have a friend who I think is in some trouble. I want you to follow her. Find out what she's doing and who she's doing it with. My guess is she's messed up with someone who's no good, and she doesn't know it. Take some notes, some pictures; find out who she's meeting and let me know. Do you think you can do that?"

"I'm not workin', so I got some time on my hands. Sure, I can do it, 'cept I don't got a camera."

"You didn't lose your job, did you?"

"Nope. I'm on leave for a week. Still coachin' the basketball team though, so I can't give the job my full attention. Got a game on Tuesday. You should come. We're pretty good."

"I've heard the team is supposed to be good." She got up from her chair. "Just spend as much time as you can on this." She got her digital camera and loaned it to her cousin. "Here's the name and address. She works at the Burton Pediatric Clinic 'til five each weekday. Her lunch is at noon. See where she goes then, and see where she goes when she leaves work in the evenings, and watch her especially on the weekends."

"It says here 'Jessie Thomas.' I got a player on my team named Thomas, lives near this address."

"That's his *mom*, Pete. You haven't ever met her?"

"I'm following *that* hotty around? That'll be fun. Didn't know her name. Sorry."

"Just follow her. I'll give you a couple a hundred bucks if you can find out who she's meeting."

"No problemo. Can't wait to get started." Pete was struggling to get up out of the low chair, so Carlee grabbed his hand and gave a helpful tug. His slimy hand slipped out of her grip, and he fell back into the chair just as Mark drilled into an electrical line and the power went out in the basement. Carlee wiped her hand on her pants leg, used both hands to grab Pete's arm, and pulled him from the chair.

"Do you smell smoke?" Mark yelled from the basement.

"You'd better get going, Pete. Mark's in the middle of another disaster. I'll probably be calling an electrician if the house doesn't burn down first."

"I'll get back with ya soon as I know somethin', Carlee." Pete put his coat back on and left the Simpson home, wondering if he was supposed to feel guilty that the house might burn down while he was driving home. He immediately started figuring, though. With an extra 200 dollars, a paycheck coming from Harding Metals on Friday, along with the first installment due on his coaching pay, he could probably get out of town and get away from Jack Harding. He was also already beginning to fantasize about watching Jessie Thomas. "Sorry, Honey. I've got my eye on a different hot babe for a while," Pete said to himself. Piggott actually *did* feel a little guilty about that. He knew he'd never really get over his *true* love, but for the time being, getting this detective job was both an exciting prospect and a good financial opportunity.

Chapter 16

Game three was a non-league affair at Mt. Morris High School. Pete had had no contact with Jack Harding since the previous Friday. It should have made him less irritable, but besides his stupidity, his most endearing trait was his bad temper, so who could be surprised that he managed to get himself tossed from a game that his team won by 28 points? His first technical foul came early in the second quarter when he called one of the three referees a "stupid, fat pig." Considering there aren't many people more stupid than the Pigman and that the overweight ref was actually quite svelte compared to Coach Piggott, it was quite an ironic statement. Once the argument was over, Coach Piggott discovered that the ref's call had actually been one that favored the Kearsley team, so it was quite an embarrassing moment for him. The second technical foul came at the horn ending the first half. One of the Hornet reserves hit a shot that would have put the team up by 19 points, but the referee waved the basket off, claiming it was shot after the horn. Piggott took off on a wild sprint across the court to shout at the ref, but he lost his equilibrium when he hurled himself off from his bench seat. He spent the better part of three seconds trying to get himself upright while running across the floor, but he lost the battle and did a belly flop a step or two past the half court circle. He bounced—twice—before skidding the final few feet into the wide-eyed referee, knocking him from his feet. The "assault" resulted in his immediate dismissal from the game. Luckily, the only physical damage done to the referee was that he was slimed by Piggott's soaking perspiration. Piggott, on the other hand, had a nasty bump on his forehead and a large floor burn on his fat belly.

Pete didn't have an assistant coach because he was self-conscious of having anyone besides his players watch him work, so the junior varsity coach had to finish the game on the Kearsley bench. Kearsley was never threatened, so everyone on the team got a significant amount of playing time. Tanner, who scored 23 points, played well in front of Sammy Moretti, who drove up from the University of Toledo to watch the game. Afterward, there was more conversation about the coach's performance than Tanner's. Coach Moretti suggested that the Thomases meet him for something to eat before he headed back to the campus. Clay was quite interested in what a Division 1 coach would have to say about Tanner's chances of playing basketball. Jessie seemed to be thinking about other things, but she was along for the ride whether she liked it or not.

***

They worked their way back to I-75 and headed south to Pierson Road, where they met again at the Red Lobster. The two cars pulled front first into adjacent parking spaces and the occupants exited their vehicles. Coach Moretti bent over and picked up what appeared to be a random piece of aluminum siding from beneath his car. He had driven over it as he parked, so he picked it up and figured on throwing it away on his way into the restaurant. When he stood, he was looking into the eyes of a teenaged boy who was pointing a Smith and Wesson .38 caliber revolver at his chest. Clay's passenger-side door was adjacent to Moretti's driver's-side door when the cars parked, so Jessie found herself standing next to Coach Moretti, looking directly into the nozzle of the gun.

"Gimme your money...all of it!" the teen yelled. He was nervously looking around the parking lot. When he saw Clay step out of his car, he pointed the gun quickly at him and then swung it back toward Moretti and Jessie, who let out a slight scream. "Shut up! You too...you gimme your money too!" he yelled at Clay while he swung the gun once again in his direction and then back again toward Sammy and Jessie. The tall black youth had braided dreadlocks and the tattoo of a chain around his neck. He seemed just as scared as everyone else, but also a lot angrier.

"We'll do what you want. There's no need to point that gun at us," Clay said, hoping to get the kid's attention.

"You first!" he yelled at Moretti. "And then you!" he yelled at Jessie, who began to cry when he pointed the gun at her.

Clay was desperately trying to figure out a way to use his mind control to get the angry kid to put down the gun. He couldn't get the kid to look at him while he was on the other side of the car, yet the teen was aiming the gun at his wife, so he quickly moved around the front of his car to get to the other side with Sammy and Jessie. If he could get the kid to look at him, he could get him to put his gun down. As he stepped around the front of his car, he found himself behind his wife and Coach Moretti. The kid saw him and pointed his gun at Clay.

"What're you doing!" he yelled.

Clay had his hands raised in the air, but no one heard him as he made eye-contact with the thief and spoke with his mind. *"Do not look away!"* he ordered the boy, focusing his mind control with a desperate concentration. *"Look me directly in the eyes!"*

The armed robber focused directly on Clay's eyes. "I'll shoot you, you don't do what I say," he said, but he sounded less angry and kind of mesmerized. "Had to shoot the last guy I robbed." His hands were shaking, but he kept his tearing eyes on Clay.

In a calm voice, Clay spoke out loud. "Put the gun down. You don't need to shoot me."

The kid was just starting to lower the gun when Sammy Moretti swung his piece of aluminum siding and chopped down on the kid's wrist. He dropped his gun and Sammy hurled his impressive bulk at the kid, tackling him and burying him beneath his heavy body. Clay grabbed Jessie and pulled her back before scrambling for the gun. As Sammy grumbled something about a citizen's arrest, Clay called 9-1-1 on his cell phone. In less than a minute, a police cruiser squealed into the lot, a police officer jumping out with his gun raised. In less than another minute he had the kid cuffed and the situation completely under control.

In the ensuing interview, Clay heard Jessie giving Sammy Moretti all of the credit for stopping the potentially violent robbery. After answering questions from the police, Sammy was interviewed by a crime reporter for the *Flint Journal*, so the Thomases said their goodbyes and left without their meal. In the car on the way home, Jessie asked Clay what he was doing behind her at the robbery scene. "He was pointing the gun at you, Jessie. I was trying to get him to focus on me instead."

"Couldn't you have done something like Sammy?"

"I did, Jessie. I distracted him, so he wouldn't hurt you."

"All I can say is that it's a good thing Sammy was there or someone might've gotten hurt."

Clay bit his tongue, fighting the urge to tell her the truth of his role. "You're right, Jess. He may have saved our lives."

***

The next afternoon, Pete Piggott picked up a newspaper at a gas station, dreading what might be said about him in the sports section. He wasn't planning on buying the paper, just reading the article. There on the front page was the headline, "Man with Aluminum Foils a Robbery." The catchy title caught his eye. As Piggott slowly worked his way through the article, he read that a teenaged youth by the name of LaDainian Hairston, a star basketball player for Hamady High, was arrested for attempted armed robbery and was the prime suspect in a robbery and attempted murder the day before. For once, Piggott actually purchased the paper and then drove by Harding Metals. He tore the article from the paper, circled the headline and the picture of Hairston, and wrote the words in all caps, "FREE INNERPRISE. SIMPEL SALES OPERTOONITY." He then stuffed the article in the business mailbox and drove away. He doubted that Harding would much care what the kid had done with his gun, but he felt better in judging the man, even if his spelling was atrocious.

Chapter 17

Two days later, on Thursday, the second week of December, Carlee got another phone call from Jessie. "I had lunch with him on Wednesday. He was *so* sweet. And he gave me flowers today. A dozen red roses. He's such a kind-hearted person, Carlee. I can't remember the last time Clay gave me flowers."

"Is everything okay, Jessie? Everything at home, I mean?"

"Sure, considering Clay only thinks about Tanner and work. And considering he did nothing to protect me from a crazed gangster kid with a gun. What could be wrong?"

Carlee, acutely conscious of the sarcasm, didn't know what to say about their adventure on Tuesday evening. She was just happy that no one got hurt. She then got right to the point. "Don't be getting too serious about this boyfriend, Jess. It'll cause nothin' but trouble. I've been there. I know."

"You've warned me plenty of times. It's not serious; it's just some innocent fun. And he wanted to be there for me after nearly getting shot on Tuesday. We just talk, but he's very caring and romantic. He gave me a necklace on Wednesday…three diamonds…very pretty…must have cost a bundle. Said he was so relieved that I wasn't hurt that he wanted to give me something special."

***

Carlee was no longer paying a bit of attention to Jessie. If she had lunch with the guy on Wednesday, she was thinking, and saw him again on Thursday, maybe Pete had some information for her. As soon as the call was over, Carlee gave her cousin a call.

"Any news?"

"Nothin', Carlee. I ain't seen a thing. The only day so far that she left the office for lunch was Wednesday. I got stopped forever by a train on Belsay Road, and when I got there, she was already gone, so all I could do was wait for her to come back to work. She had a big smile on her face, but that's all I can tell ya."

"Nothing else to share?"

"Nope. Had a game on Tuesday and late practice after the girls' team today, so I wasn't there when she left work. I drove by the house after practice today, and she was home. Monday and Wednesday, she went right home, and I never saw her leave again."

"Okay. Keep at it, especially Saturday."

Pete Piggott wasn't any help so far. The only days Jessie had done anything, he had managed to miss it. Carlee was going to have to be patient.

***

Clay got home from an evening math class at about 8:30 PM. There, sitting on the kitchen counter was a dozen roses. Clay had noticed a bracelet a couple of months back, and over the last few weeks, he'd noticed a designer purse, a necklace, and now some flowers. There had been no credit card purchases that indicated that she bought the bracelet, purse, or necklace. When going through her purse, looking for receipts, Clay came across a plain black Tracphone. There were no numbers stored, and if there had been any incoming or outgoing calls, records had been deleted. There was no evidence of any calls.

When Jessie entered the kitchen, Clay said, "Hi, Jessie. Who are the flowers from?"

John. Clay could have sworn he heard her say, "John," but she was clearly saying, "I got them when I stopped at the store for a few things. They were really cheap, so I bought them." Clay was very focused on what his wife was saying, and it was disturbing to him that he could have sworn she said, "John."

112

"They're nice. It's been a while since I bought you flowers. I'm sorry."

"Yes, it has." Jessie scooped up a pile of mail and headed away.

Clay watched her extraordinary butt as she walked away to the bedroom, and then his mind began to wander as it had been doing a lot lately. On Wednesday evening, he had just by chance happened upon the television show, *The Mentalist*. As part of the show's introduction, a definition was presented. "Mentalist. N. Someone who uses mental acuity, hypnosis, and/or suggestion. A master manipulator of thoughts and behavior." Clay looked up *mentalist* on-line, and one thing led to another, but he took special notice of the field of parapsychology. After taking notes, he continued, and discovered that there was a neuroscientist at the University of Michigan in Ann Arbor who specialized not only in the field of neuroscience but also in the field of parapsychology. Tanner's powers had Clay thinking that it was time for him to learn a little more about what was going on, maybe get some answers to his questions. Hearing "John" in his head made him convinced even more that there were things he needed to know. And Jessie's behavior was concerning him too. He needed to get things right, and maybe finding some answers to his questions would be a step in the right direction. He was going to give Dr. Zander Frauss a call.

***

Johnny Papalli had given Jack a call on Thursday. He had done his research and was proposing his bet. Kearsley would be playing a home game on Friday against the Clio Mustangs. Clio was probably the weakest team in the league. He proposed two separate 2,000 dollar bets—both, he felt, giving an advantage to Jack. Both of the men were criminals, but though Johnny was better at it than Jack, he resisted the urge to bury Jack under his growing debt. There was no sense at the moment in getting under Jack's skin. Johnny knew that even if he lost both bets, he would still get the legitimate 4,000 dollars that Jack owed him. He knew that Jack's weakness was anger, and he didn't see any point in drawing his ire over inconsequential high school basketball games. There were other criminal investments that were a higher priority for Johnny. Since he was attending the games anyway, he was just having a little fun at Jack's expense. So Johnny saw his proposal as a no-lose proposition. The first bet was that Kearsley would win by at least thirty points. The second was that Tanner Thomas would get a triple-double, recording double figures in three separate statistical categories, such as points, rebounds, and assists. Jack agreed immediately, knowing he had no chance of losing either bet. He had big plans for Tanner Thomas.

During the school day on Friday, one of Jack's "employees" was to dump a 64 fluid ounce bottle of Mrs. Butterworth's original thick-n-rich syrup into the gas tank of Tanner Thomas's sport red metallic 2006 Pontiac Grand Prix. If everything went according to plan, the car would stall on Tanner's drive home, somewhere between the school and his house, and Jack's men would be waiting.

***

After school on Friday, Tanner hung out with his friends for about an hour. The girls' team was having a shoot around in the gym, a very casual practice, and the coach let Tanner and Luke Simms get some shooting in too. While shooting a set of ten free throws with Tanner, one of the girls, Lacey Winfield, who stood just short of six feet tall, happened to look Tanner in the eyes. *"Try to dunk it, Lacey."*

Tanner tossed her a pass, and instead of shooting another free throw like she was supposed to do, she took off dribbling, jumped her highest, and barely touched the bottom of the net as she "threw down" her dunk. The sheepish look on her face cracked Tanner up. When it was Tanner's turn to shoot ten shots, he really started having fun with Lacey. After he made his first shot, he thought, *"Chest pass."* Lacey fired back a two-handed chest pass. After his second shot bounced in off the front of the rim, he thought, *"Bounce pass."* Lacey bounced him an accurate bounce pass. Tanner's third shot spun through the net and he thought, *"Pass it off your forehead."* Lacey slammed the ball off her forehead, and

114

after four bounces, Tanner picked it up and prepared for his fourth shot. His shot hit the bottom of the net and this time he thought, *"Spin in a circle and pass it behind your back."* Lacey caught the ball, spun completely in a circle and passed the ball behind her back sideways, nowhere near Tanner.

Her coach happened to see the missed dunk and the silly passes and had had enough. "What're you doin', Lacey? Either you get focused or I turn this 'shoot around' into a run around. You wanna get some shootin' in or some *running*?"

"Shooting, Coach. Sorry. I'll get focused."

Tanner couldn't help but continue to laugh as he finished his set of ten, only making three of his last six. He thanked Lacey and her coach for letting him get some shots, said, "See ya" to Luke, and he headed for his car. He'd head home, do about 15 minutes of math homework, get some food, maybe take a short nap, and get ready for the game. He was already excited to play.

As Tanner started up his car, a truck about four rows over also started. The parking lot was mostly empty, but Tanner didn't notice that the truck was following him as he pulled out of his parking space and headed home. He turned onto Genesee Road and headed south toward Richfield Road. As he got about a mile and a half down the road, the car started to sputter, then stalled. Tanner flipped on his hazard lights, coasted to the shoulder of the road, and when the car came to a stop, he tried to restart it. It would fire, but wouldn't start.

A truck pulled up behind Tanner and stopped. A man parked his gray Chevy Trailblazer and stepped out of the vehicle. He was wearing brown leather gloves, a tan overcoat with the collar turned up, a navy blue sports coat and a tie, and a classy brown Dobbs style dress hat with a bow band and a tight brim. He had on sunglasses. His face was friendly, though, and he looked concerned. "Is something wrong?"

Tanner looked the stranger over. He didn't recognize him, but he looked friendly enough. "The car just stalled on me, and it won't start."

"Do you have someone to call?"

"Both my parents will still be at work, but I could call and see if they could help."

"Listen, I've got a AAA card. I could get a tow truck here in just a few minutes. We can have your car towed to a service station, and I could give you a ride home…that is if you don't live a hundred miles away." He said those words with a smile.

"Lemme call my dad first." Tanner used his cell phone to call his father, but there was no answer. He left a message to call him back. "Okay, I guess yours is as good a solution as any. Thanks," Tanner said to the friendly man.

Within minutes everything was arranged. M-15 Towing would pick up the car and deliver it to Church and Sons Auto Repair on Davison Road in Burton. Tanner called his dad again and left a message that the car would be at the repair shop and that he had a ride home. The driver of the tow truck was instructed to drop the car off at the repair shop and Tanner's dad would come by to decide what to do with it. Once all the details were taken care of, Tanner hopped into the front seat of the Trailblazer and told the driver to go to Davison Road and take a left.

The driver pulled out onto the road and within seconds a hard metal object was thrust into the back of Tanner's neck. "Don't say a word," came a voice from the backseat. A gun barrel was poking into his neck from under the raised front seat headrest. "If I shoot you in the back of the neck, you'll probably die, but if you happen to live, you'll probably never walk again."

"What's going on?" Tanner managed to squeeze out of his throat.

"Just what you think. Kidnapping. Keep your eyes looking forward, Kid." From behind Tanner's seat, he got on his phone, punched in a number, and said, "We got 'im." At that exact moment, Tanner sent an outgoing call to 9-1-1 from his own phone, hoping to somehow communicate his need for help. He wondered if there was a way to trace his location through his cell phone. The kidnapper immediately ended his call, however, and said, "Put this blindfold on…and don't make any stupid moves."

Tanner nervously ended his call and turned his phone quickly to silent mode, expecting a return call from 9-1-1. He then wrapped the blindfold over his eyes and, with somewhat shaky hands, tied it. He asked, "Why are you doing this?"

"I hear it's payback, Kid. Somethin' 'bout payback more'n 20 years overdue."

"I'm only 17 years old. What do you mean more than '20 years overdue'?"

"I guess you're not the one bein' paid back then, Genius. Now shut up and do as you're told."

The driver and Tanner never said another word. Blindfolded, Tanner couldn't see a thing, but he could *feel* his heart beating, and the gun never quite stopped feeling cold against his neck. The kidnapper with the gun was the only one to speak while Tanner silently rode out the short drive to their destination, worrying about what was going to happen next.

Jeff La Ferney

Chapter 18

Jack Harding had planned his kidnapping to perfection. He figured that he'd done as much as 2,000 dollars damage to the Thomas car—that evened things up a bit. He'd hold Tanner throughout the game, assuring that he'd win 4,000 dollars on his bet. Then he'd request a ransom from Clay Thomas for maybe ten grand more. He really didn't want to hurt the kid, but he wanted to put the family, Clay in particular, through some mental anguish, anguish like Jack had experienced in high school. The kidnappers were hired from out of town, so no one should recognize them, and the plates on the truck were stolen from a nearly identical Chevy Trailblazer, just in case a cop rolled up during the roadside emergency. The kidnappers were to take Tanner to a foreclosed rental property that Jack had once owned, but currently was owned by First Financial Credit Union. The abandoned house, which had been sitting empty for at least four years, was nowhere near Harding Metals, and Jack still had working keys. They would arrange towing services through a stolen AAA card. Jack felt confident that there was no way he could be incriminated if something went wrong. The kidnappers didn't even know his name, just a number to call to verify their "pick-up." He had an ironclad alibi as well. He made sure a whole bar full of people noticed him when he bought a round of drinks for everyone on hand. The only thing left was to head to the game, watch his son take over now that Tanner Thomas wouldn't be playing, and gloat over his winnings when the game ended.

***

Pete Piggott was in a great mood as he followed Jessie Thomas from work to home at 5:15 Friday evening. She didn't make any stops and Pete pulled away and headed back to the gym. He'd grab a couple of McDonald's burgers and be at the gym easily before the JV game began. He hadn't had to talk to or see Jack Harding all week; Jack had left Pete alone completely. Pete would have to head back to work after the game, but he was looking forward to the fact that he would be able to coach the game without feeling Jack Harding's interference. They would be playing Clio, which should be an easy win. Nothing had happened all week with Jessie Thomas, but he looked forward to every visual encounter with her; she was one hot woman.

***

Jessie pulled into the driveway, a little surprised to not see Tanner's car. He took his games very seriously, and it wasn't like him to not be at home going through his regular pre-game routine. She thought about calling John, but thought twice about it. She didn't want it to look like she was chasing him; he was supposed to be chasing her. It was a good thing she didn't call because Clay barged in unexpectedly just then.

"Hi, Jessie. I'm in a hurry because I've got to go check out Tanner's car before we leave for the game."

"What's wrong?"

"Tanner had some car trouble. His car was towed to Church and Sons Auto Repair. Tanner!" he called. "Tanner, I need to talk to you!"

Tanner didn't answer. "I wondered where his car was," Jessie said. "Tanner!" She headed for his room, but his room was empty, and within minutes it was obvious he wasn't in the house at all.

"Where could he be?" Clay wondered aloud. He called Tanner's cell phone, but there was no answer. He called TJ, but she didn't know where he was. He called Mike Powell and then Luke Simms, but no one knew anything. Luke said he'd left school at about 3:30; that was the last time he saw him.

Clay left Jessie at the house in case there was a call, and he headed the short distance to the auto repair shop. They claimed that they hadn't seen Tanner. The car was simply dropped off by M-15 Towing. Clay raced to the service station. The tow truck driver was there and explained that Tanner had left with a man that he assumed was Tanner's father. He drove a gray Chevy Trailblazer, newer model, '06…'07, maybe. The guy was dressed in a tan overcoat, sports coat, white shirt, tie, hat…. "Company AAA card, I recall. Signed it…let's see…" He pulled a clipboard from a counter top. "It's signed 'Clive Cussler'."

"Oh, no."

"What?"

"Clive Cussler's an author. He just made that name up. Tanner's in trouble."

"I don't know. He seemed like a real nice guy."

"But my son still isn't home, and I got a call from him at about quarter to four. It's almost six o'clock now, and he has a basketball game tonight that he wouldn't be missing on purpose."

Clay left and punched in his home phone number. "Is he there?"

"No, and he hasn't called," Jessie answered. "What's going on?"

"I don't know, but I think we need to call the police. I think he's been kidnapped."

**

Clay dialed 9-1-1 and headed home. A police officer pulled into his driveway as Clay was getting out of his car. By 6:30, a full report was written up. The detective, Lance Hutchinson was his name, was starting to explain the policy about a person being missing for at least 24 hours when Clay very calmly and very clearly looked him in the eyes and thought, *"You are going to ignore your policies. This is a kidnapping, and it is urgent!"*

"However," the detective explained, "in this case we will ignore the policy. This definitely appears to be a kidnapping and deserves our urgent attention."

"That's what I was thinking," said Clay honestly.

"Here's my card. I'll be working this case. If there's any news, call me. Oh, and call me Hutch."

Jessie was nearly frantic as the police car pulled away. Clay put his arms around her and tried to assure her that everything would be okay.

***

The kidnappers, fortunately for Tanner, weren't mistreating him. They pulled into a garage, lowered the garage door, led him into a house, and sat him in a metal chair. Tanner's ankles were not tied, but his wrists were secured behind his back. The kidnappers weren't rough as they also tied him to the chair. With his hands behind him, however, Tanner couldn't get his blindfold off, and if he couldn't get his blindfold off, there would be no way to use his powers of mind control, not if he couldn't look into their eyes. In the car, he had settled himself a bit, thinking he could manipulate the men, but when they left the blindfold on, he started getting nervous again.

The two kidnappers pulled out a deck of cards and sat patiently awaiting any new orders. "Just sit tight, Kid. Don't try anything, and you won't get hurt. Our orders were to hold you for the evening. We're to be paid tonight when our replacements come, and then we'll be on our way. Let us know if you need a drink or need to use the facilities." The talkative kidnapper laughed when he used the word *facilities.*

They were playing gin—five dollars a hand. When the quieter kidnapper, the driver, won the first hand, there was discussion about what the bid would be for the next hand. The quieter one wanted the bet to be five dollars again, but the talkative one with the gun wanted to go double or nothing. They argued briefly before the driver gave in. Since both bets were the same, Tanner realized they weren't the smartest men in the world, and he began to have hope of escaping them…if only he could get his blindfold off.

After that hand, they played two more, double or nothing, the more talkative kidnapper yapping continuously, and the quieter one winning every game. He was now up 40 dollars. Tanner asked, "Could you tell me what time it is?"

"Time for you to shut up," the gunman replied, obviously irritated about his losses.

"6:45," the other man said. "Ignore him; he's just a bad loser."

Tanner was getting anxious. Game time was generally around 7:30. He'd barely have enough time to get out of the house, get home to get his things, and get back to the gym in time for the game, even if they let him go right then. As he puts those thoughts together, he actually got mad. The men were arguing again about their bet for the next game when Tanner focused in on the direction of their voices and with great concentration thought, *"You need to let me go."*

"We should let the kid go," the driver said.

"Yeah, we really should. If we could, I'd do it," the kidnapper with the gun replied.

What? Did he just get into their heads? He decided to try again. *"Get out of that chair right now, and untie me."*

"Why don't we just untie the kid; he ain't goin' nowhere," the driver suggested.

"I don't have a problem with that." So one of the men began to untie him.

"I need you to give me the truck keys. Just put them in my hand."

As soon as his wrists were freed and he was released from the chair, an ignition key and remote were placed in his right hand. It occurred to him that he'd never seen the man with the gun, and the other man was practically disguised behind the hat, glasses, and coat collar. He'd never be able to identify either of them, and they would know it. Tanner was scared but so angry about possibly missing his game that he was focused and actually thinking quite clearly.

"Now, lead me to the garage. I won't take off the blindfold until I'm in the truck, so I'll never be able to identify you."

"Keep the blindfold on the kid 'til you let him go," the kidnapper with the gun said. "Don't take it off 'til you get in the truck, Kid. You'll never be able to identify either of us, and we'll be long gone before anyone looks in this dump."

"Lead me to the truck door. Open the garage, step back in the house, and let me go."

"Sorry for the trouble, Kid," the driver apologized. "Once you get in the truck, we'll open the garage door and step back in the house. Then you can go." Then almost as a second thought, he said, "You sure don't talk much, Kid."

"I do have a request before I go. Tell me your phone number," Tanner commanded.

Amazingly, the gunman looked at his disposable cell and replied, "313-818-4444."

"Thank you," Tanner said, and then he felt his way into the vehicle.

Once Tanner was in the truck, the electric garage door opener pulled the door up. He heard the kidnappers close the door to the house, so he pulled off his blindfold, backed out of the garage, and drove away.

"I can't believe you just gave him the phone number," the driver said.

"Heck, it's a prepaid phone. We wipe it down and dispose of it. No way to trace it to us. What the heck just happened?" the gunman asked incredulously.

"Looks to me like we just screwed up a kidnapping."

"That's what I was thinkin'. I'm also thinkin' we need to clean up the house and get our butts outta here," the gunman said.

***

Once on the road, Tanner immediately pulled out his cell phone. It was ten minutes to seven. He called home.

"Tanner! Are you all right?" Tanner could tell his dad was worried.

"Yes. I was kidnapped, Dad, but I'm okay. I just want to get to my game on time. Dad, I'm not sure where I am right now. It's some road called Western, but I know I'm not far from where the car broke down...Wait, here's Richfield Rd. I'll be home soon; I have their truck, and I'm hurrying. Would you get my basketball gear ready?"

"You want to *play*?"

"Dad, I'm all right. I wasn't hurt at all…a little scared, maybe, but I'm okay, and I want to play."

"Tanner! Are you okay, Honey?" Jessie had grabbed another phone. She was crying.

"Mom, I'm okay. I'll be home in just a few minutes."

When Tanner pulled into the driveway, his parents ran out to meet him. Jessie was bawling, and Clay couldn't stop his own tears from running. There were hugs and kisses. It was nice to be home, but Tanner wanted to get to the school. He could forget the whole ordeal once the game began. Jessie was overreacting and Clay was fumbling along, trying to get the family together and into the car. Tanner's bag was ready.

Jessie wailed, "Oh, I forgot my purse…you two wait just a minute!"

***

Once in the car, Tanner tried to explain about the breakdown and the ride he'd accepted. Jessie tried to scold him, and then thought better of it. Tanner explained that the kidnappers had been hired to hold him through the evening, but all of a sudden they just decided to let him go. Jessie was so relieved that she started crying all over again. She was sitting in the back seat with Tanner, holding his hand.

Clay had questions that he couldn't ask while Jessie was in the car. Instead, he focused on Tanner's eyes through the rear view mirror, and he heard, *My powers worked even though I was blindfolded.* Clay quickly looked at Jessie to see if she had heard what he had heard, but she obviously hadn't. She didn't ask any questions about "powers" and "blindfolds." That meant, Clay realized, that he had pulled that thought from Tanner's mind. He had read Tanner's mind, and Tanner had demonstrated mind-control without eye contact! What was going on? Why would their powers somehow be increasing?

Tanner grabbed his bag with warm-ups, uniform, shoes, ankle braces, etc. and ran into the school once the car arrived. It was 7:20. He charged into the locker room and the team was still sitting, waiting for the JV game to end. Fortunately, the game was lasting longer than usual.

Coach Piggott walked up to Clay and nearly shouted, "Where in the heck have you been?"

"I was kidnapped, Coach. I escaped, and I got here as fast as I could."

Several teammates started laughing, but they could see that Tanner was deadly serious, and the laughing stopped abruptly.

"You expect me to believe that?"

Tanner looked him in the eyes and thought, *"You believe me. I was kidnapped."*

"Oh, heck, I actually believe you were kidnapped, Thomas. This has been one heck of a year so far. Get your stuff on. We hit the floor in a couple a minutes." Pete Piggott, who had thought this one game was going to run smoothly, once again realized this was going to be a year of continuous trials. When Tanner Thomas didn't show up, he just chalked it up to another bad break—more bad news. But several players, Luke Simms and Mike Powell in particular, had told him that Tanner was missing. To find out that he was kidnapped was par for the course this year. At least he was here now. It was going to be nice being able to play him just the way he wanted.

Chapter 19

When the varsity Hornets ran onto the court, Jack Harding was at the concession stand. He was in a great mood, chatting it up with anyone willing to talk. Clay and Jessie paid and entered the stands without his notice. Jessie was holding onto Clay like she was afraid to lose sight of him. When the horn sounded to end warm-ups, the players lined up on the court for the National Anthem. Jack made his way among the fans and paid no attention to the basketball team, arms around each other's shoulders, warm-up jackets still on. The crowd clapped after the Anthem, and to mild applause, the public address announcer went through the starting lineup of the Clio Mustangs. Then the lights went down and the spotlight swooped toward the Kearsley Hornet bench.

"Starting at one forward, at 6'2", number 33, senior, Mike Powell...Starting at the other forward, at 6'3", number 42, junior, Luke Simms...Starting at center, at 6'6", number 44, senior, Tommy Monroe...Starting at one guard, at 5'11", number 21, senior, Kevin Harding...And starting at the other guard, at 6'2", number 23, senior, Tanner Thomas!" The crowd roared its final approval as Tanner Thomas took the floor, spotlight following his run to shake hands with the referees and Clio's coach, and finally to join with his teammates at half court. Jack Harding sat in shock. How could something like this happen?

"You really get kidnapped today?" Kevin asked Tanner as they took the floor for the jump ball.

"Yep."

"And you're okay to play?"

"Kevin, let's just kick these guys' butts. It's time to play ball right now. I'm okay; let's just play ball." Tanner made those remarks with such pure intensity that Luke, Mike, and Sprout overheard, and each of them geared up for one special game.

Sprout tapped the opening tip to Mike, who zipped it to Tanner, who lofted it to Luke, who laid it in for a two-point lead—three seconds, no dribbles, two points. On Clio's first possession, a Mustang player tried to complete a cross-court pass, but Tanner intercepted it, took three dribbles and passed to the right wing to Kevin, whose three-pointer hit nothing but net. After the basket, the Hornets dropped back to their half-court man-to-man defense. A Mustang shot finally went up after a half-dozen passes and Tanner leaped high for the rebound, snapping it down with his right hand, and slapping it into his left. Immediately, he was on his way down the court. He looked to his right, crossed over with amazing quickness to his left, and entered the lane. As the last Clio defender stepped up to stop Tanner, he slipped a short, quick pass back to the right to Mike Powell, who laid it in for two more points. Now down 7-0, Clio set up its offense a second time, and on a drive from the wing, Sprout got a small piece of the shot. It still managed to catch a little rim, but Tanner came down with the ball. A whistle was blown when a Mustang player was called for a reach-in foul. Luke passed the ball in bounds, and Tanner set up the Kearsley offense, holding up two fingers. Monroe set a high screen, and Tanner used it to drive to his right. Sprout rolled down the lane and received a slick behind-the-back pass from Tanner. Monroe took one step and slammed down a two-handed dunk. Clio's coach rose to call a time-out, but the ball was passed in before the official acknowledged it. Tanner stole the pass and converted a left-handed lay-up. The Mustangs got their time-out after Thomas's basket, but after five possessions each player had scored and Tanner had two points, two rebounds, two steals, and four assists. Kearsley was ahead 11-0. The players hollered and slapped fives all the way to the bench. The route was on.

There was a 40 point lead and a running clock by the time the fourth quarter started. The final score was 87-42, a 45 point victory. Powell had a career-high ten points. Kevin Harding had 16, Luke Simms had 15, and Sprout Monroe had 21. Tanner Thomas finished with 12 points, 12 rebounds, seven steals, and a school-record 17 assists—he had finished with a triple-double. Jack Harding's plan went up in smoke. Tanner could not be held for ransom, he emerged as a greater leader and greater star than at any other time in his career, and Jack had lost an additional 4,000 dollars. What was supposed to be a momentous time of revenge turned out to be just another bad day for Jack Harding. He was steaming mad as he left the bleachers and headed out of the gym, making only one quick glance over his shoulder at Clay and his pathetic wife, who was clinging to his arm. He was going to have to go back to the drawing board if he wanted his revenge on Clay Thomas.

***

Clay finally remembered to call Detective Hutchinson at halftime of the game. He called again from the school once the game ended, and "Hutch" and his partner, John Janski, were waiting in their driveway when the Thomas family returned home. Hutch went into the house with the family while his partner continued talking on the police radio. Tanner began his story once again, describing the driver as best as he could, but knowing he'd never recognize him because of the hat, coat, and sunglasses.

"He didn't seem suspicious to you when you first met him?" the detective asked.

"No, the sun was shining, and it was windy and cold. There was nothing suspicious about how he looked, and he was friendly and helpful."

"Well, we've already tracked down the AAA membership card. The owner, who lives in Wayne County, checked his wallet for his card, and it was missing. He hadn't reported it because he hadn't realized it was missing. We have a handwriting sample from when your kidnapper signed for the tow. Clive Cussler is obviously made up. We also now have the vehicle that Tanner drove home."

"Excuse me, Hutch," the partner entered the house and interrupted. "Dispatch says the license plates don't match the vehicle. Plates were stolen from a different gray Trailblazer in Inkster. The truck in the driveway was driven off a used-car lot, a dealership off Telegraph Road in Dearborn. Seems a college kid was taking the truck for a test drive. When he returned, some guy in a Tiger's jacket and hat grabbed the kid's truck key right out of his hands and drove away. We'll impound the vehicle and check for prints or other evidence."

"Thanks, Janski. Oh, and check the abduction site. Genesee Road between Old Genesee and Thorntree." Hutch turned his attention back to Tanner. "Anything else to add, Tanner?" Hutch asked.

"Janski and Hutch?" Tanner smiled.

"Nice to see you have your sense of humor still intact," Hutch replied as he rolled his eyes and smirked. "It's Hutch and Janski. Anything else you remember?"

"Just after he pressed the gun to my neck, he made a phone call. I called 9-1-1 at exactly the same time. I was going to keep the call open, but I didn't. You'll know the exact time he made the call though. The dude said, 'We got him,'" Tanner informed the detective. "Maybe you can trace the call, somehow. I have the cell phone number…"

"*What? How*'d you manage that?"

"Um…you're prob'ly not gonna believe this, but I asked him for it, and he gave it to me."

Hutchinson had quite a skeptical look when he asked, "What is it?"

"313-818-4444."

"Had to be lying to you, but check it out," Hutch told Janski. He turned back to Tanner. "Did you see where they took you?"

"No, but I know the general area. Maybe I could find it again. When they let me go, I didn't know where I was, and I was trying to get away…in the dark."

"Do you know why they took you?"

"He said it was 'payback…more than 20 years overdue.'"

"Does that make sense to any of you?" Detective Hutchinson asked the family, but no one had a clue.

"Well, we'll be looking into this. We'll let you know. Call if you think of anything else. We'll probably have a man following you around for awhile, until we get this figured out."

"Do you think those men will come after Tanner again?" Jessie wanted to know.

"I don't think so, Mrs. Thomas. Those men *gave* Tanner the truck key, gave him their phone number—maybe—and let him drive away unharmed. It's the guy who hired those men that we'll be looking for. He's the real kidnapper."

After fingerprinting Tanner to eliminate his prints from any pulled from the truck, the policemen were escorted to the door and out of the house. The family, seated together on the living room couch, took another minute to thank the Lord that Tanner was safe. None of this made sense to anyone.

***

When Tanner finally pried himself away from his mother and went to his room, Clay managed to look in for a moment. "You used your powers without eye-contact?"

"How did you know that?"

"Believe it or not, I read your mind in the car."

"I thought you couldn't do that?"

"I didn't know I could, but I think it's happened twice now. I'm going to visit a neuroscientist tomorrow at U of M. I'm hoping to get some answers. No matter what's going on here, Tanner, the most important thing is you're safe. We love you."

"I love you guys too, Dad. It's good to be home."

Jeff La Ferney

Chapter 20

Clay got up early on Saturday morning. Jessie and Tanner were both still in bed when he left at 7:00 to visit Dr. Zander Frauss. Dr. Frauss was a neuroscientist for the University of Michigan's Department of Psychiatric Medicine. What had caught Clay's attention when he did some research was that Dr. Frauss headed the parapsychology laboratory called The Division of Perceptual Studies. The good doctor seemed more than happy to meet with Clay at 8:00 AM and answer some of his questions.

"Good to meet you, Mr. Thomas," Dr. Frauss said while gripping Clay's hand in a firm handshake. "Have a seat, please." Frauss had a pleasant smile to go with his strong, confident handshake. He had blond hair with a few strands of gray, but he looked to be no more than in his mid-forties. He was clean-shaven, was wearing a casual sweater and a pair of khaki pants. He didn't even have glasses as Clay imagined a scientist would wear. He simply was not what Clay was expecting. The office had family pictures, sports paraphernalia, and a limited number of books. The one book on his desk was a Bible. They both sat down in comfortable leather chairs facing each other. "What can I do for you?"

"Well, I hope I'm not wasting your time, and mine as well, for that matter, but I have some questions. As I told you on the phone, I stumbled upon your name while doing an Internet search."

"Yes, I recall."

"May I ask what exactly you do as the head of a parapsychology laboratory?"

"Of course. I, and my staff, basically do research and experimentation in the field of parapsychology. I am a neuroscientist first. I'm hired by the University, but occasionally I've earned government grants to do studies in the field of neuroscience or any of its related sub-fields, of which parapsychology is one."

"So you are a believer in people having mental powers?"

"As a scientist, I would never accept the ideas of parapsychology by faith alone—a 'believer'—as you say. These mental powers that you suggest would have to have scientific substance for me to be a 'believer.'"

"Have you discovered people with mind-powers in your research?"

"Of course."

"Many?"

"No, not many, and usually those with quote, 'powers,' have raised more questions than answers. I work under the assumption that there is a scientific, identifiable, medical reason that a person exhibits parapsychological powers, but I've yet to come across anyone who has strong enough powers to prove any of my theories. Several are simply mentalists, like in the TV show. They have great mental acuity, intelligence, and/or skills of observation, which allow them to manipulate thoughts and behavior. They can appear to know more about a subject than they really do. Cold readings and hot readings are examples of this. Through our tests and experiments and studies, we occasionally find evidence that people display actual parapsychological abilities, but the abilities always seem to be weak and inconsistent."

"Do you feel the powers are demonic in some way?" That was a question weighing on Clay's mind.

"Mr. Thomas, I believe in the occult. It's real. I'm a born-again Christian, and I'm certain that Satan rules this world and that there are dark practices at work, but that is not what I'm talking about here. For some reason, there are people that have *extra* mental abilities. That is what I'm talking about. There are people who can do things with their minds. Their brains work better than other people's brains. We've done scientific research, and I'm convinced from the field of neuroscience that there are people who get better use of their minds than others."

"Can you give examples?"

"I could give you dozens, but it's time I asked *you* a few questions, Mr. Thomas."

"Please, call me Clay."

"Of course, Clay. Now you tell me. What have you experienced that leads you here? People don't come to see me simply to satisfy curiosity. People come to me because they believe they've had some sort of parapsycological experience. So what's yours?"

Clay never expected Zander Frauss to take the offensive. He wasn't sure what to say. "I'm not sure if I'm in a position to talk about it, Dr. Frauss."

"Please, call me Zander."

"Okay." Clay couldn't help but smile. "Zander, may I explain by using hypotheticals?"

"If you wish."

"Just in case you somehow think I'm talking about myself, who else will know about this conversation?"

"I promise you, Clay, as God is my witness, what you say in this room, stays in this room. I've had more people than you could believe sitting right where you are in this office, all of whom have had some sort of experience, and most of whom have no true parapsychological abilities. I listen and I advise. You talk, and I'll listen. Then you can decide if you would like to talk some more."

"Okay, Zander." Clay took a deep breath. He had never discussed with a sole, save Tanner just about a week and a half before, what he was about to discuss with Dr. Zander Frauss. "Suppose someone claims that he...or she...can influence what people think. He...or she...can put thoughts in a person's mind and make them do or say or feel or even forget whatever he wants. Do you believe that is possible?"

"Is this person especially intelligent?"

"Let's just say the person is above average."

"Did this person ever have any trauma to the brain or any special circumstance that may have influenced the neurology of the brain?"

Clay had to think about that one. Neither he nor Tanner had ever had a concussion that he was aware of. "You mean like a concussion?"

"Possibly, but more likely a neck/spinal injury or something like a period of time where the brain was starved of oxygen, like a strangulation and resuscitation. Did this person ever have to be revived?"

"What if he…or she…had?" Clay tried not to give evidence of the chill that went through his body.

"Well, our research seems to indicate that those people who actually show genuine abilities have much more active brain activity in the medulla oblongata. That's the part of the brain associated with autonomic functions, which affect the heart rate, digestion, breathing, perspiration, dilation of the pupils, urination, and even sexual arousal, for instance. Whereas most of its actions are involuntary, some, such as breathing, work in tandem with the conscious mind. The medulla oblongata is thought to be in two parts. One part is open and one part is closed. We've found that in people with special mental abilities, the closed part is at least partially open, caused generally by spinal cord trauma or some sort of trauma caused by strangulation. With both parts open, these people receive 'super' autonomic functions, in a sense. As I said, most autonomic functions are involuntary, but some, like breathing, can be conscious or unconscious. A person can make himself stop breathing or blink or hold his urine, for instance. Our research seems to indicate that persons with special mental abilities are getting additional sensory information through the medulla oblongata, those 'super' autonomic functions I mentioned. Their brains are inputting data that mine isn't. But the kicker is, they are somehow able to *control* that input. They can control objects or control thoughts of others or control what thoughts they can read, for instance. The control is what makes them special. So, did this person ever have spinal trauma or strangulation?"

Clay was dumbfounded. He didn't even know what to say. He decided to take a leap of faith and confide in the man. "Forget the hypotheticals, Zander. Both my son and I almost died at childbirth. In both instances, we were strangled by our own umbilical cords and emergency resuscitation was needed. In both cases we almost died, and in both cases our lives were saved but parents were warned of possible brain damage. Thankfully, there was no brain damage; instead, we both have above average intelligence, like I said. But are you suggesting that our unusual childbirths may have caused abnormalities in our medulla oblongatas?"

"I haven't suggested any such thing. We'd have to have an MRI to see if there are any irregularities, and I don't know of any parapsychological abilities in either you or your son. Are you suggesting you have some?"

"Without question, Doc, we both have mind-control powers."

Jeff La Ferney

Chapter 21

Jessie finally awoke at about 11:00. Tanner, like a normal teenaged boy, could sleep the rest of the day if allowed. But while he was still sleeping, she made a couple of phone calls. First, she called John and told him about Friday night's adventure. He sounded genuinely concerned and asked if she'd like to see him. She declined, saying she needed to stay home with Tanner. Next, she called Carlee. Carlee was shocked. She said she'd make up some lunch for her and Tanner and would be over to the house soon. She claimed that getting out of the house was just what she needed. Three college coaches called, but Jessie said Tanner wasn't available, and she took messages. Around noon, Clay still wasn't home, and TJ had come to visit. Tanner was just getting out of the shower.

Pete Piggott had done a couple of drive-bys to stake out Jessie, but he saw the police cruiser sitting in front of the house each time, so he finally decided to go home before he became a suspect in the kidnapping. A policeman would be wondering what he was doing there. Besides, he was tired. After the game, he had gone back to work for the first time in a week. Jack never made an appearance, so the night went smoothly, but it was a cold, windy night, and those kinds of nights seemed to suck the energy from Pete. He headed home and went to sleep.

***

Back at the University of Michigan, Clay and Zander continued their discussion. When Clay so confidently stated that both he and his son had mind-control powers, Dr. Zander Frauss sat up with interest.

"Are you willing to explain?" Zander asked Clay.

"Do you want me to prove it to you?"

"Can you?"

"Without question. Give me a pen and some paper," Clay said. Zander gave him a yellow writing pad and an ink pen. "Okay, I'll write something down. Then I'll use my mind to tell you what to think. You say what pops into your head, and then I'll show you what I wrote."

"Okay, I'm with you."

Clay scribbled on the writing pad, "Pickles are sweet like candy."

"Okay." Clay turned the pad over. "Look into my eyes, Zander. When I get done talking, I'll tell you what to think. You say it out loud, then I'll show you what I wrote. You ready?"

"I'm ready."

Clay stared intently into Dr. Frauss's eyes. *"Pickles are sweet like candy."*

"Pickles are sweet like candy," Dr. Frauss said out loud. Clay turned the pad over and showed it to Zander. He looked genuinely amused. With a smile, he said, "Let's do that again."

Clay turned to the next page and wrote, "All birds run on four legs."

"Okay, Zander, look me in the eyes. *All birds run on four legs.*"

"All birds run on four legs," the doctor stated. Clay showed him the exact words, written on his paper. "That's pretty impressive. Let's do that one more time."

Clay took the paper and wrote, "I love the Michigan State Spartans." He stared into Dr. Frauss's eyes and thought, *"I love the Michigan State Spartans."*

"Clay, the words that just popped into my head, I refuse to say," he said with a smile.

"Say out loud, I love the Michigan State Spartans!" Clay ordered the doctor.

"I love the Michigan State Spartans… I *told* you I wasn't going to say that…"

"I *made* you say it. I'm telling you, I've been able to do this for probably the last 30 years."

"Incredible. You didn't just put the thought in my head, you made me say it. And Tanner…your son can do this too?"

"Last night Tanner was kidnapped. While *blindfolded* he made two kidnappers untie him, give him the truck key, tell him their cell phone number, and let him go. I've never manipulated a mind without eye contact, but Tanner can do it, and he's only been aware of his power for the last three months. Why do you think it's taken so long for him to discover his power and such a short time to develop it?"

"There's no way to answer that question unequivocally. It's possible he's had it longer but not known. Another theory might be that he's had a slower development in the medulla oblongata. We've also theorized, with little or no proof because we haven't had enough test cases, that when two people with parapsychological abilities physically spend time together, their powers increase. Have you had any increase in your own abilities?"

"Um, actually…yes. I believe so. Two times in the last two days I believe I've read a person's mind."

"Explain what you did."

"Well, in both instances, I was *very* focused on the desire to know something. In both cases, I was looking into the person's eyes, just like when I plant thoughts, and in both cases, I'm sure I heard words that weren't spoken out loud. Tanner confirmed last night that I had read his mind. The other situation, I don't know if I'll ever know for sure."

"Clay, let me run an MRI and see if your medulla oblongata is open significantly in both parts, then we can run some other tests to see if you have additional powers."

"Like what?"

"Like psychokinesis, ESP, precognition, clairvoyance, or hypnosis. It seems you have abilities with mind-control and telepathy; maybe you have others. We can test Tanner too."

"Listen, Doc. I, *we*, don't want to be lab experiments. I don't want anyone to know what I can do. I don't want anyone to think I've influenced any thoughts and decisions. Does that make sense?"

"How about just doing the MRI for now? We've got a machine right here in the lab. I can run it myself. I'll look at the results and let you know. What we've talked about will stay in this room if that's what you want. If and when you change your mind, I'd like for you to come to me. We can do any other tests whenever you are willing. As a matter of fact, I'd like for you to call me if you have any other questions." Dr. Frauss hesitated, then looked at Clay as if something had just registered in his brain. "Your son was kidnapped yesterday?"

"A lot of weird things are happening lately."

Clay ended up allowing the MRI. Afterward, he grabbed his coat, shook Dr. Frauss's hand, and left the office. Frauss would have the results within a couple of days and would give Clay a call. As he pulled out of his parking space, it began to rain. Clay's windshield wipers swung back and forth, barely touching the glass and leaving streaks of wetness on the windshield. He could barely see where he was going and he had about an hour's drive. Clay found himself saying out loud once again, "I hate rain."

***

Carlee showed up with a dish of spaghetti, a side of meat sauce, and a side of alfredo sauce. She had a bag of bread and a tossed salad that she bought at the deli at the grocery store on the way over. She asked how Jessie and Tanner were doing and then actually *thanked* Jessie for the opportunity to provide the meal and get out of the house before Mark drove her crazy.

"What's going on over there this time?" Jessie asked. She knew the kind of disasters that Mark could create, and she figured a good story was about to be told.

142

She told about how her husband, Mark, had gotten up early in the morning. There was a small leak in the basement wall, and he was determined to fix it before the rain rolled in that was predicted for later that afternoon. "He needed to dig a hole outside large enough for him to tar the outside wall," she explained.

"Oh, no. I'm sensing trouble already," Jessie interjected. "It's one disaster after another," she explained to TJ, who wasn't familiar with Mark Simpson's escapades.

"Just wait," Carlee giggled. "This one is hilarious." She continued to explain that he'd been digging for several hours in the hard ground before he finally got impatient. "Now, this hole wasn't nearly big enough for him to get down into it," she described, "but he figured he'd just reach down there anyway and tar the wall as best as he could." She was laughing now, and there were smiles all around. Carlee continued to explain that while he was reaching down into the hole to slop tar on the crack, he fell into it, head first. "Remember, this hole wasn't nearly big enough for him to climb into, so it was impossible for Mark to pull himself out of it." Everyone was laughing now. "Angela and Heather found him, feet sticking in the air, yelling for help." The three girls weren't tall enough to lift him out, so after several unsuccessful tries, Carlee, holding onto Mark's ankles, had to use a ladder to climb up while Angela and Heather held most of his weight. "You should have seen him when we finally pulled him out, tar all over his face, hair, shirt, and hands. I've no idea how he's gonna clean the stuff off. That man's gonna kill himself one day!"

By the time Carlee had finished the story, everyone—Tanner, TJ, Jessie, and Carlee— were laughing so hard there were tears, and the day after Tanner's kidnapping didn't seem so terrible. Great friends, great food, and stories of Mark were enough to brighten the day.

Jeff La Ferney

Chapter 22

Monday, Jessie went to work, but was miserable. Her heart wasn't into it. She was concerned about Tanner at school even though she was assured that a policeman would be following him. A tired Pete Piggott, who only had a short nap after work, waited for her at lunch and followed her home after work, but nothing happened. Tuesday, Jessie called in sick, deciding to get a little rest and do some heavy thinking. When Pete parked across from the clinic to watch for a lunch rendezvous, her car wasn't there, so he figured he'd missed her again. He clearly wasn't too good at his private eye job. He waited for her to return from her lunch, and when she still hadn't returned at 1:30, he decided to drive by her house. She was just pulling into the driveway as he arrived. She had been to lunch with John.

They had simply sat in a parking lot together, eating Hungry Howie's subs that John had ordered to go. John listened to her story about Tanner with keen interest. Somehow the kidnappers had simply let Tanner go. He'd never heard anything so strange. Jessie explained that the police were watching over Tanner and that they were investigating information concerning the cell phone number that Tanner gave them. The stolen truck was at the police impound lot, being searched for evidence. They were unsure of the location of the house that Tanner was taken to. John listened intently, holding Jessie's hands and occasionally gently wiping small tears from her eyes—an intimate act that didn't escape Jessie's notice. He was the perfect gentleman, the perfect person to talk to and be with while going through a hard time. Finally, he gently kissed her, a kiss that became quite passionate. Jessie found herself giving in to the man that obviously cared so much for her. When John finally pulled away, he said, "I'm falling in love with you, Jessie."

When Jessie didn't respond, her heart beating rapidly and her thoughts swirling, John apologized. "I'm sorry. I shouldn't have said that. The timing is terrible with what you've been through, and I promised to never pressure you. Please forgive me."

"It's okay. I'm just not sure what I think right now. I know I care about you, and I appreciate you being here for me. I just need to think about things some more."

***

When Jessie returned home and entered the house, there were two messages blinking on the machine. The first was a request from Detective Hutchinson for Clay to call. They were still working on the phone information, and they had pulled some physical evidence from the Trailblazer. The other message was much more disturbing. "Clay, this is Zander Frauss from U of M. I have your test results. Please give me a call. 734-764-1234." Jessie didn't know if she should be worried or angry about that second message. Out of curiosity, Jessie dialed the number.

"Good afternoon. Dr. Frauss's office. Substitute secretary, Dixie, speakin'. May I help you?"

"May I speak with Dr. Frauss, please?"

"He's not been in the office since lunch time, Honey. Is there anything I can help you with?"

"Um, well, my name is Jessie Thomas. I have a message from Dr. Frauss asking to call about test results for my husband, Clay Thomas. Is there any way I can find out the results?"

"Well, I'm just a fill-in for the day, Ma'am, so I don't think I can help ya…Wait a minute. What'd you say yer husband's name was?"

"Clay Thomas."

"His chart happens to be sittin' right out here on the desk."

146

"Is there any information that you could give me? I'd really appreciate it."

"There's some pictures and such in here that I don't think I'd be much help with, but there's a sticky note that says, 'MRI test results positive. Both parts medulla oblongata completely open. Call Clay.' That's all it says, Honey, and I really can't understand much else on the chart. I'm just fillin' in for his regular secretary. I was told he'd be back in the office tomorrow, though."

"Medulla...what?"

"'Both parts medulla oblongata completely open' is what it says. I hope I've answered yer questions, Sweety. Is there anything else I can do for ya?"

"No, thank you. You've been very helpful."

"You're welcome. You have a nice day now."

As she hung up the phone, Jessie considered once again that Clay wasn't communicating with her about important parts of his life. After the kiss from John, she was beginning to doubt whether their marriage was going to survive much longer.

Jeff La Ferney

Chapter 23

Tanner left a message on his cell phone for his father to call him as soon as school got out on Tuesday. There was something important that he needed to talk about. At 2:45, Clay called Tanner, who suggested that his father come to pick him up right away. About 20 minutes later, Tanner climbed into Clay's Pontiac G8, and they zipped out of the parking lot followed by an officer from the Burton Police Department.

"What's up, Tanner?"

"I had a dream last night, only it was more than a dream. I dreamed about the house that I was taken to. Dad, it seemed like the house was calling to me. I can't explain that exactly, but in my dream or vision or whatever it was, I could see myself blindfolded in a metal chair. It was in the corner of a small living room, which had nothing but four metal folding chairs, two TV tables, and a lamp. The green curtains were closed, and the only light was the lamp sitting on the floor. Across the house, in a kitchen, two men were sitting at a card table, playing cards with gloves on. It was like I was seeing through the blindfold, so everything was kind of blurry. All of a sudden, the men got up, untied me, and placed a key in my hand. They led me through the kitchen, opened a door to the garage, and led me to the truck. I got in and then the garage door was raised. It was dark outside, but in my dream with the blindfold off, I could clearly see the numbers 1486 sort of glow over the front doorway. When I drove by the first street sign, it said, 'Delta Drive.' I turned on Epselon Trail and drove away.

Dad, I'm certain I was seeing the house I was taken to. It's at 1486 Delta Drive."

Clay stopped the car along the side of Daly Boulevard, the street exiting the school. He entered 1486 Delta Drive on his GPS and waited for the gadget to search for a satellite. When the location was discovered, he drove off again, police car following. In about ten minutes, they were sitting outside the house. "It looks just like the one in the dream," Tanner nearly whispered. "The numbers are over the door just like I saw."

They climbed out of the car and were met by the policeman who had followed. "Is there something wrong, Mr. Thomas?" he asked.

Tanner responded. "This is where they took me. This is the house that I escaped from."

"Are you sure?" the officer asked, but Clay knew he was sure. He'd been doing a lot of research in the field of parapsychology. Clairvoyance, he recalled, was the ability to gain information about an object, person, location, or physical event through means other than known senses. Maybe the house was literally "calling" to Tanner or maybe God had given him a vision. Maybe Tanner somehow had a new power to discern and comprehend information that his senses had somehow overlooked four days earlier. Clay didn't fully understand how his son received the information, but he was certain that Tanner had led them to the exact site in which he had been held hostage.

"I'm sure," Tanner answered. "This is the place."

The policeman called Detective Hutchinson to give him the information, and he spoke with Hutch for several minutes. "Hutch says that we'll need a warrant to look inside, but we should be able to get one, based on Tanner's certainty that this is the house. He wants me to stick around and knock on a few doors. He'll find out who owns the house. We may just catch your kidnapper yet."

"Did he say anything else?" Clay asked.

"He said the only clear prints on the steering wheel belonged to Tanner. Other prints were only partials or were smudged. That makes sense knowing that the driver wore gloves. There are other prints in the truck, but remember it was a stolen, used vehicle, and any number of people could have been in it. We're assuming that both men wore gloves, though. Except for a roll of duct tape, which the kidnappers never used, there was nothing else in the truck that would be incriminating—unless we catch them. If we catch them, which seems unlikely, there could be any number of fibers or hairs or other clues to help convict them. Hutch said for me to stick around here and ask the neighbors a few questions. He'll have someone keep an eye on Tanner at the game tonight. He thinks we should still keep close for a while."

***

On the way home, Clay explained that Church and Sons had called and that it looked and smelled like someone had dumped a large quantity of maple syrup in Tanner's gas tank. It would probably cost 1,500 to 2,000 dollars to clean everything up. Except for the deductible, the insurance company would pay for the vandalism. It might be another week before the car would be ready.

***

Though the season was young, the ballgame on Tuesday night was supposed to be Kearsley's toughest game to date. The Fenton Tigers, who were 3-0, were hosting the 4-0 Hornets and were expected to be the most likely spoiler of Kearsley's league championship. Word was spreading fast after four games that Tanner Thomas was even better than advertised. He was averaging almost 23 points along with nine assists and seven rebounds per game. He was an unselfish leader, excellent student, and had shown he had the size and athletic ability to possibly play Division 1 ball. Both Michigan and Michigan State had sent assistant coaches to watch the game, and the head coach from Central Michigan University was also in attendance. It was a good crowd at Fenton High School for a Tuesday night. The pep band was enthusiastically playing in the stands, creating additional pre-game energy and excitement.

Early in the game, Fenton surprised Kearsley by running a match-up zone, something they hadn't done at all when Coach

151

Piggott had them scouted. The Hornets took a little time adjusting, trying to determine whether to run their man or their zone offense. Eventually, Tanner and his teammates began to control the tempo of the game. Tanner, Kevin, Luke, and even Lance Mankowski were draining three-pointers at a high percentage, and as they started to build a lead, Fenton was forced to spread out their defense a bit, which allowed Tanner to penetrate and make some nice passes. What was supposed to be a close game eventually turned into a 23 point route. Tanner took just 12 shots, hitting five of eight from three-point range and three of four on shots in the paint, one of which he was fouled on and converted into a traditional three-point play. He made three of four other free throws and ended with 25 points. He also had ten assists and four rebounds.

Each of the coaches took a moment to speak with Coach Piggott, who seemed delighted by the attention. Clay had to laugh as he watched all three men wipe their right hands on a pants leg after shaking hands with the Pigman. Not one of the men lingered, each taking advantage of his first opportunity to escape. All three spoke briefly with Tanner and his parents, offering kind words. Jack Harding would have certainly been jealous, had he not missed the game entirely. He had a couple of business meetings and then went back to his office to try to figure out some new way to hurt Clay Thomas. He wasn't one to give up easily.

***

At home, Clay sensed that something was bothering Jessie. She was distant and uncommonly untalkative. She obviously was taking the kidnapping hard and was worried about Tanner. Clay told her that Tanner had led the police to the house that he was held in by the kidnappers, and he told her about the information he had received about the truck at the impound lot.

"I forgot to tell you there was a message to call the detective, but I guess you found out what he needed to tell you anyway," Jessie said.

"They're a couple of pretty good clues. Hopefully they can figure out who set the kidnapping up. They seem to think it's unlikely that they'll locate the men who did the actual kidnapping."

They both slipped into bed without more conversation. Clay kissed Jessie goodnight as he had for more than 19 years, and Jessie rolled over and went to sleep.

Chapter 24

The following afternoon, Clay decided to give Zander Frauss a call from his office at the community college. His regular secretary answered and then transferred him to Frauss. "Hello, Clay. It's good to hear from you. I take it you got my message?"

"What? No, I didn't get any message."

"I called your number at home yesterday morning and left a voicemail to call me about the test results."

"Why would you do that? I *told* you I didn't want anyone to know about what we talked about. You told me that what we talked about would stay in your office."

"I never mentioned anything specific in the message. I take my patient confidentiality seriously, but I told you that I would call when I had the results from the test."

"My wife doesn't know anything about this, Zander, and I would have liked to keep it that way."

"I didn't know that you're married. You never said a word about a wife in my office."

"I have a son, Zander," Clay said sarcastically.

"Believe me, that doesn't mean you have a wife. You never spoke of one. Shouldn't that have come up?"

"You may've screwed up, Frauss. She must've heard the message. That might partly explain how she was acting yesterday if she thinks I'm hiding something from her."

"I'm sorry for the mix-up, Clay. But she shouldn't know anything except that I have your test results."

"I never wanted to tell her," Clay admitted. "I've always feared how she'd react."

"I'm sorry, Clay, and I'm sure this isn't a good time to bring this up, but are you going to bring Tanner in for an MRI? Your results showed both parts of your medulla oblongata are completely open."

"It isn't necessary, Doc. He's got the same thing going that I do, except stronger, I think. I'm pretty sure he's also clairvoyant. The house the kidnappers held him in called to him, and he found it."

***

That night, as they lay in bed in the dark, Clay put his arms around Jessie. She noticeably stiffened, but didn't resist. Clay started nibbling on an ear, then repositioned himself to kiss her. She turned away. "Not now."

"What's wrong, Jessie?"

"Nothing…everything…I don't know."

"The police are working on the case, and Tanner's safe. They're watching him every day."

"Of course I'm worried about Tanner, Clay. I love him with all my heart, but there's more wrong than just problems with Tanner." By then she had escaped Clay's grasp completely.

"Okay, tell me…I'm listening."

Jessie took a deep breath. She almost said, "Never mind," but she'd been stewing ever since the phone message the day before, so she said, "What are you hiding from me, Clay?"

"What do you mean?"

"You're *always* hiding something from me. You have been since the beginning. It always seems like you're lying to me."

"I don't lie to you, Jessie."

"Yes, you do. You won't look me in the eyes—even when we make love. You're hiding something, Clay. I see it every day. You carry around some inner pain or some inner secret, and you don't share it with me."

"If that's true, it's because I don't want to hurt you."

156

"Hurt me? Are you kidding? You hurt me every time you hide something from me. You hurt me when you ignore me. You hurt me when you refuse to make decisions over and over again. You hurt me when you have problems and you don't share them with me. The longer we're married the *more* you hurt me."

"I'm sorry. I didn't know. I love you, Jessie. I wouldn't hurt you on purpose."

"What are you hiding now, Clay? Are you in pain? Are you sick? Is there some reason you visited a neuroscientist?"

"I'm not sick or in pain. You can stop worrying about that."

By now, Jessie was sitting up in bed. "Then tell me why you visited a neuroscientist?"

"No. You can't possibly understand why."

"Try me. Tell me about Zander Frauss and your MRI."

Clay hesitated. He'd been dreading this conversation his whole married life. Were his worst fears about to be realized?

"He left a message on the phone yesterday," Jessie continued. "I called his office and managed to get a secretary to give me information. You had an MRI. His notes said that both parts of your medulla oblong something or other are completely open. Tell me what that's about!"

"I had some tests done…I'm fine. There's nothing to worry about."

"Look at me, Clay. You're not telling me the truth. I looked up that brain thingy and read about it. I looked up Zander Frauss too. I learned about parapsychology. I read about his tests and his 'Division of Perceptual Studies.' Tanner was kidnapped on Friday, and on Saturday you had something so important to do that you left us here and were gone half the day. And now you're telling me there's nothing to worry about? Are you sure you don't lie to me, Clay?"

"I think it would be a mistake to tell you what's going on. I don't think you'd understand."

"Then you don't love me. If you loved me, you wouldn't hide things from me. You'd have more faith in me…You wouldn't *lie* to me," she stressed.

"I'm not lying to you. Yes, there's something that I think is best that you don't know." Clay began to think about mind-control. Maybe he should make her stop asking questions, but he put the thought immediately out of his mind.

"Then tell me. Tell me what you're hiding. Tell me why you had an MRI and what's wrong with your brain."

"I can't do that. You wouldn't understand. If *you* loved me, you would trust me on this one. Please trust me."

"I'm not so sure I *do* love you. I've been wondering about that for quite some time now." Then Jessie grabbed her pillow and a blanket and began to leave the room. Clay reached for her, but she pulled away and exited. She threw herself on the couch and began to cry. In the room, Clay cried as well. He knew now that he had to tell her his secret—Tanner's secret too, and he couldn't imagine the discussion turning out well, but if he didn't tell her, he knew he had lost her for good.

Chapter 25

The next morning Clay asked Jessie to make arrangements to go in to work late. He drove Tanner to school but didn't tell him about the conversation he was about to have with Jessie. Kids don't need to know when parents are fighting. Besides, he had enough on his plate already—new powers, a kidnapping, a basketball scholarship, school, girlfriend, basketball team. Clay would tell his son later, once he saw Jessie's reaction.

Back at home, Jessie simply sat on the couch and stared out into space. Clay knew the conversation would be difficult, so he said a quick prayer and then began. "I went to Dr. Frauss because I had questions that I thought he could answer." He paused to see if Jessie was listening.

"What questions?"

"Good, you're listening." Clay continued to wait until Jessie turned to look at him. "I saw something on TV that led me to do some research on the Internet. I stumbled across Zander Frauss's name. As I guess you know, he's a neuroscientist, but what I found most interesting was that he headed a department that specialized in parapsychology. Parapsychology is a discipline that seeks to investigate the existence and causes of psychic abilities using the scientific method. Frauss is a scientist that does studies and research about psychic abilities." Clay paused again.

"And what does that have to do with you?"

"It has to do with me *and* Tanner." It was the moment of truth. "We both have forms of psychic abilities."

First Jessie simply laughed. Clay didn't flinch. Then she seemed to at least consider what he had just said. "What's your 'psychic' ability, Clay? And what's Tanner's?"

Clay took a deep breath. He said, "We both can control minds. Tanner is better at it than I am. And lately it appears that maybe I can read minds too, and Tanner shows signs of being clairvoyant."

"And why should I believe what you're saying?"

"Because you asked me to tell you the truth, and the truth is that we both have special powers."

"How long have you two had these powers?" Jessie still didn't believe. This wasn't going well.

"I'm pretty sure that I've been able to control minds since I was about ten years old. Tanner's been able to do it for about three months."

"Okay, I'm pretending that I believe you. What does this scientist at U of M have to do with anything?"

"By the time I was about 12 or 13, I was sure I could control people's minds. Once I figured out what I was doing, I messed around with the power, but I knew it would never make me happy. It's a curse, Jessie; I swear it's a curse. Anyway, I've almost never used the power for the past 20-plus years. But I started seeing things with Tanner that made me believe he was controlling minds too. Once I was certain, I confronted him, and I was right. I went to Dr. Frauss for answers. I wanted to know why we could do the things we could do."

"And?"

"Well, he believes it has to do with the medulla oblongata. The medulla oblongata has two parts, one that's closed and one that's open. In his studies, he determined that those with actual psychic powers had a medulla that was at least partially open in both parts. He said the abnormality occurred generally because of spinal cord trauma or strangulation. Tanner and I both almost died at childbirth because of strangulation from the umbilical cord. Once I demonstrated to him that I actually had abilities, he convinced me to have an MRI to look closely at my brain. I guess the test confirmed that my medulla oblongata is fully open in both parts. It would be a safe guess that Tanner's is too; he has more power than I do."

"How do you know that?"

"Tanner escaped his kidnappers using mind control. He told the men to let him go, to give him the truck key, to give him their phone number. He did it while blindfolded. I can only do it with eye to eye contact. Yesterday afternoon, Tanner found the house that he was held captive in. He had a dream that led him right to it. That's clairvoyance, Jessie."

Jessie was being very patient; it appeared to Clay that she was thinking deeply, like she was giving grave consideration to his words. Gradually, Clay began to see a realization growing in her eyes, and he knew she was getting to what he feared most.

"This is real?" she asked.

"Yes."

"You can manipulate minds?"

"Yes."

"Have you ever messed with *Tanner's* mind?"

"Besides to make him talk to me a couple of weeks ago, only one other time."

"When was that?"

"This is stupid, Honey, but it was at a family reunion. You were smiling it up in a rainstorm, and it made me mad. I told Tanner to hate the rain."

"*That's* why he hates the rain?"

"I'm sorry. I've told him over and over since then that it's his choice to like something or not. He doesn't have to hate rain just because I do. But he's never changed his opinion."

"You're such a jerk! And I suppose you've controlled *my* mind too?" Bingo! There it was—the realization that Clay had feared his entire marriage. "Have you ever told *me* what to think?" Jessie demanded.

"Once. One time, Jessie, I swear. When Tanner was born and you were told you could no longer have children, I made you believe that it was okay; you were blaming yourself for the tragedy and that you wouldn't be able to have more children. I didn't want you to feel that way, so I told you to accept that it wasn't your fault. I convinced you that it wasn't your fault."

Jessie paused like something was bothering her...like there was something in the back of her mind that she was trying to reach...like there was more on her mind than the argument that they were having. Finally she snapped out of it and the emotional Jessie reemerged. "Do you expect me to believe that? *One* time in twenty years?"

"It's the truth."

"You never made me do or believe anything? How about sex, Clay? Did you ever make me have sex?"

"NO! Never!"

"You never raped me, Clay? Did you happen to tell me to love you? Is *that* how we ended up together?" She was becoming a raving lunatic.

"No, Jessie, no. I've loved you too much for that. I'd have to look you in the eyes to practice mind control. I would look away to be sure not to influence you. I wanted you to love me because you *chose* to love me, so I never influenced you in any way. What joy would there be in *making* you love me? What kind of relationship would that be? I've lived our whole marriage in fear that you would find this out and think exactly what you're thinking now. No, I never influenced your choices—not ever!"

"I don't believe you, Clay. How can I believe you? You've been lying to me for 20 years. I can't believe you, and I truly can't stand you right now. I need you to get out of here. How could I ever love you again?"

"Think about it, Jess. When have you ever done something that you didn't want? When have I looked you in the eyes and told you what to do? I never have, and if you really think about it, you'll know it's true. You even said that I never look you in the eyes. Please, just think about it." Clay then started for the door, but he turned back. He wanted to ask, "Who's John?" but instead he simply said, "I may have saved your life when that kid was pointing that gun at you. I made him listen to me, and I got him to lower his gun before Sammy jumped him. I protected you because

I love you. I always have, and I've let you make your own choices."

"Leave, Clay. I don't think I believe you, and I want you out of here."

Chapter 26

Pete Piggott pulled up to the Burton Pediatric Clinic at eleven in the morning. He was doing so poorly on his stakeout job that he decided to arrive early enough that he was sure not to miss Jessie again if she happened to leave for lunch that day. Once again, however, her car was already missing from the lot. After her conversation with Clay, she had called back to the clinic and called in sick. Piggott, just for the heck of it, so he could tell Carlee how hard he was trying, drove by the Thomas house, and just as he approached their address, the garage door went up and Jessie began to back out. Piggott's heart started racing and his palms started sweating more than usual. Except for bashing his passenger side mirror into the neighbor's mailbox, he somehow managed to drive by the house without further incident. He turned around in a different neighbor's driveway and began to follow Jessie as discreetly as a no-talent detective possibly could without losing her altogether.

Jessie pulled into the Super 8 Motel on Dort Highway, and Pete Piggott finally snapped his first picture—it was of the motel. He snapped a second one of Jessie sitting in her car, talking on a phone, and his third of her stepping out of the car—it was quite a good shot of her with the motel in the background. She walked directly to room 12—another picture was taken. The door opened right into the parking lot, and Jessie walked directly in, an act that Pete also caught on film. Piggott, so focused on the job at hand, was unaware that he wasn't the only one taking pictures.

***

Jessie stepped into the room and right into the arms of her boyfriend. The motel was a dump, but she didn't care; she just wanted to see John and be held by him. The morning conversation with Clay and the kidnapping of Tanner had her needing some comfort, someone to make her feel secure.

"What's wrong?" John asked.

"No questions right now. Just hold me. I need you to hold me," and Jessie kissed him. She pressed herself hard against him, taking a break only to whisper, "I want you."

John led her to the bed, even as they kissed, and lowered her to the mattress edge. Jessie gave no resistance as he undressed her. John took complete control of the situation, something that Jessie found especially exciting. She gave herself to him completely and willingly, and he took full advantage of the passion of the beautiful woman on the bed beneath him.

***

When they had finished and Jessie was as physically spent as she was emotionally, she began to weep. John was a little unsure of what to make of the tears, but he went to her and put his arms around her. "Do you want to talk?"

Jessie grabbed her underwear, broke away, and went to the bathroom to rinse her face and regain her composure. When she returned to the room, John was sitting on the bed, fully dressed. Jessie sat in the chair opposite the bed. She needed to talk, to talk to someone she could trust, so she decided to start right in.

"I kicked Clay out this morning…told him I wasn't sure I loved him anymore."

John resisted the urge to smile. "Did something happen?"

"He's been lying to me, lying for over 20 years. He says he didn't want to hurt me, that he loves me, but I just can't accept that. Not right now. Not with you in the picture."

"I don't know what you're talking about. Explain…please."

"There was a message on our machine Tuesday. It was from some neuroscientist at U of M. He said something about an MRI. Clay never told me about an MRI, and when I confronted him, he

166

wanted to avoid the topic. I pushed him, wouldn't let it go. He told me that he was meeting to have some questions answered about his 'mind-control' powers, powers that Tanner supposedly has too. The MRI was a test the doctor ran."

"Hold on now. You're saying your husband believes he can control people's minds?"

"Says he's been able to do it since he was a kid. He says Tanner has been able to do it for just a few months, but he's better at it than Clay."

John felt an anger building up inside him. "That manipulative jerk! He's been able to manipulate," he paused to get control, "to manipulate you your whole life? Do you believe it?"

"He claims he's used the power on me one time. One time only."

"But he's had this 'power' since he was a kid?" John seemed to be having a hard time getting a grasp on what she was saying, but at the same time, he seemed to be getting angry.

Jessie was looking into his eyes, and she didn't like what she was seeing. There was a fierce anger there, anger above and beyond what she had expected. She had a quick flashback to Carlee warning her about his temper. She had just made love to him, and now he was scaring her.

"What is it, John?"

"He's been manipulating people his whole life! Who knows how many times he's gotten into people's heads! Who knows what kind of havoc he has wreaked in his lifetime! He may have even told you to love him, for all you know."

Seeing him angry like this made her feel compelled to defend Clay. "I don't think so. He says he didn't. He seemed sincere. I want to believe him."

"He doesn't love you, Jessie. He doesn't love you like I do." He walked to Jessie and grabbed her; he pulled her out of the chair and started kissing her. But there was still that anger in his eyes. Jessie tried to pull away. He grabbed her arms and squeezed too tightly.

"You're hurting me. Stop!"

"Tell me you love me, Jessie. Tell me you love *me*!"

"You're hurting me. Let go!"

She jerked away, and John released her. Jessie had kicked a man out of her house who loved her, a man that had the power to make her love him back, and yet he claimed he never did, that he would never take her choice away. And now she was in a motel room with another man, someone whose arms she'd run to, someone she thought she was falling in love with, and he was *telling* her to love him. He was angry, and he was scaring her. "What has gotten into you? I can't tell you that, not right now. I can't believe you would try to make me say it." She started gathering the rest of her clothes up, and then she headed for the bathroom and locked the door. She began to cry again. She thought that she heard the motel room door open and close, and after waiting for other sounds, she was convinced that John had left the room. She finished dressing, reapplied some make-up, and opened the door. The room was empty.

***

Pete Piggott had waited outside the motel room for nearly an hour and a half and was getting hungry. Just as he began to wonder if the motel office might let him use their restroom, the door to room twelve opened, and Pete's hairs literally stood on end. Pete, while working at Harding Metals, had come across some pretty shady people, some pretty bad people. He knew some people in the city of Flint that he would have been shocked to find were having an affair with someone as fine as Jessie Thomas, but the one person who would have shocked him the most was standing outside the Super 8 Motel, room number 12, right then. Pete snapped several pictures. The man drove away, and eventually Jessie Thomas exited the room. He had his hand in his coat pocket, feeling the metal of the .22 caliber handgun as he watched to make sure she safely got in her car. As she pulled away, Pete followed temporarily, just to be sure she got away from the motel safely. By doing so, Private Eye Pete never saw a different man enter the vacated motel room. He was carrying a small bag, and he had a camera hanging from his neck.

168

Chapter 27

Pete went to Walmart to print the pictures and then began calling Carlee. After many hours and several attempts, at eight o'clock that evening, he finally got an answer. Heather answered the phone. She explained that her mother was at the hospital, and she gave Piggott her mom's cell phone number.

Carlee answered the phone on the second ring. "Hello."

"Carlee, it's Pete. One of the twins gave…"

"They're not twins, Pete."

"Well, one of your daughters gave me your number 'cause I've been tryin' to reach you all day. Said you were at the hospital. You all right?"

"I'm okay. Mark's not in such good shape."

"What happened?"

"Well, he was working in the garage—more heaters and lights and saws and what not going at the same time than you can imagine. He didn't just trip a breaker, he literally completely blew the fuse for the garage. So now the garage door opener doesn't work. I needed to get my car out, so Mark lifted the door manually for me. He was just standing there, and it crashed back down right on top of his head. Knocked him completely unconscious. He fell, and then the door fell on his leg and trapped him on the floor. By the time we got the door up and Mark pulled away, he was conscious but pretty woozy. I brought him to emergency to check for brain damage. Figured he had a cracked skull and a broken leg, but all he has," she said sarcastically, "is *another* large knot on his head and a minor concussion. The leg is fine too. Maybe it knocked some sense into 'im, though. Sure hope so, anyway. He thinks he's Tim the Toolman and acts just like him... You ever gonna have some news for me?"

"Yeah, I got some all right. I got some pics to show you. You're not gonna be happy. When can I bring them to you?"

"We're gonna be here a while, I think, so bring them over sometime tomorrow afternoon."

"Do you want me to keep following her?"

"Do you think you need to?"

"You asked me to find out what she's doin' and who she's doin' it with. I got that figured out."

"Then you can stop. Call me tomorrow at home."

***

Clay stayed late and was going to have to spend the night in his office. He'd see Jessie at Tanner's game the next day for sure, but he hoped for another chance to talk to her before then. He was worried who John was and what was going on, but whether Jessie had strayed or not, he knew he would love her anyway. He wanted their relationship to be right, so if Jessie could choose to love him back, he would certainly overlook anything she had done wrong. He had been able to forgive her before, so he knew he could do it again.

Before the evening was over, however, Clay began to feel incredibly anxious and unsure of himself, so he decided to give Tanner a call. He explained to Tanner about his trip to U of M and his meeting with Dr. Frauss. He tried as best as he could to explain about the research that Frauss had done in the field of parapsychology. He told about the medulla oblongata, and the theory that their traumatic childbirths had opened their medullas to some extra sensory abilities. While most of the human race cannot control those abilities, somehow Clay and Tanner could. Clay explained that there are other abilities beyond mind control like ESP or telekinesis or clairvoyance, among others. He believed that Tanner had experienced some sort of clairvoyance when he found the house. "I believe I've experienced at least two examples of

170

telepathy—I've read a person's mind. Dr. Frauss theorizes that our powers are improving and expanding because we are close to each other."

Tanner accepted the explanation without question. That was the easy part of the conversation. The hard part was to come. "Dr. Frauss called the house on Tuesday. He left a message and your mother started asking questions. I had to tell her, Tanner. She knows."

"Did she freak out?"

"She threw me out of the house. She figures I've been lying to her our whole marriage. She figures I've been manipulating her for 20 years."

"You told *me* you haven't! Didn't you tell *her*?"

"Of course, but she wasn't listening. Remember when I told you about the girlfriend in high school that I made like me? There was no joy in that. I vowed I'd never do that again. If someone loves me, I want to know that they love me of their own volition. I swear to you, Tanner. I've never forced her to love me."

"She'll get over it, Dad. It's a lot to take in. You were right when you said that these powers in a way were a curse. I'm starting to understand what you've gone through your whole life."

"I've been praying it'll all work out. Maybe you should too. I'm going to try to drop by the house tomorrow after you leave for your game. Maybe she'll talk to me again tomorrow. I'll let you go, Tanner. Good night…and it sure is nice talking to someone."

"It's nice talkin' to you too, Dad. G'night."

Jeff La Ferney

Chapter 28

Pete called Carlee Friday afternoon after getting a little bit of sleep. She was home and asked him to stop over. He put his gun, illegal activity as it was, back in his coat pocket. He no longer felt comfortable without it. He gathered his pictures up and headed for Carlee's, arriving about 15 minutes after the phone call.

"How's 'Tim the Toolman'?" Pete asked, showing only the second hint of humor that anyone's ever recognized.

"Sleepin' like a baby. *Finally*, peace in the house for a change. Can I get you something to drink?"

"Coffee'd be good if ya got it. Got a brutal headache."

They continued some small talk while Carlee poured a cup for her cousin. Eventually they got down to business. "So what'd you find out?"

Pete extracted the pictures from the photo envelope and returned her camera. "Took these yesterday afternoon."

After flipping through the photos, she asked, "You think she's having an affair with this guy?"

"I know I missed a couple a meets. This is the first time I got evidence. She drove up alone, made that call…" He pointed to a picture. "Then she got out the car and walked right into room 12." He pointed to another picture. "Was in the room for an hour 20, maybe an hour and a half, and then *he* walked out of the room." He pointed to yet another picture. She walked out after him maybe five minutes later."

"You told me I wasn't going to be happy. You know this guy?"

"Yeah, I know him all right, and it's not good news. He's a crook. He's controlling and selfish and mean and as lowdown bad as a man can get. Can't see what a babe like that would see in him."

"What's his name, and who is he?"

So Pete told her.

***

Carlee called Jessie. There was no answer at home because she was back at work again, and her cell went directly to voicemail. Carlee simply told her, "Jessie, we need to talk about your boyfriend. It's an emergency. Call me back." Pete Piggott had told Carlee to keep her 200 bucks. He didn't want any more part of the craziness. He was truly worried about Jessie, and that had scared Carlee.

***

After wasting time around the office, Clay called Jessie's cell phone as well. No answer—straight to voicemail. His message was, "I've talked to Tanner and told him what we talked about yesterday. Please let me talk to you before the game tonight. I love you, Jessie."

***

John also called Jessie late in the afternoon. He called her prepaid phone, however, and left a message. "I'm very sorry about getting angry yesterday. There's no excuse. I have something special to give to you if you would meet me. I know your son has a game tonight. Please come by my office after the game, so we can talk again. Yesterday should have been very special—actually part of it was very special. I'd like a chance to redeem myself. Please come after the basketball game."

***

The University of Michigan head basketball coach called Clay at his office and identified himself.

"Hi, Coach. I appreciate the call. What can I do for you?"

"I wanted you to know that we're very impressed with Tanner, impressed enough that we're giving a lot of thought to offering him a scholarship. We think he'd fit into our system nicely, and our point guard is graduating. We'll be needing a replacement, and we think Tanner's a good candidate. Do you think we could set up an appointment to get together with your family and Tanner? Just to talk. Get to know each other better."

"Sure, Coach. I'm sure we can arrange that. I think Tanner would be really interested in meeting with you."

So they set up a meeting time. Not everything was going wrong in their lives. Big Ten, Division 1, full-ride…it was exciting to think about.

***

Detective Hutchinson was accumulating evidence. First Financial Credit Union owned the house that Tanner had identified. It had been a rental house starting about five years back that went unoccupied for close to a year. Then approximately four years ago, the owner, with no rental income, simply turned the house over to the bank to get out from under the debt. The house, Hutch discovered, was a foreclosed property that had been sitting unsold for nearly four years. However, the name of the previous owner raised some eyebrows.

It wasn't easy, but someone on the investigative team who had more techno-smarts than Hutch also managed to get some interesting information from phone records. Based on the exact location and the exact time of the call—which Tanner had pinpointed when he made his 9-1-1 call—the detective was able to determine that the kidnapper's outgoing call came from a prepaid phone purchased in Inkster, Michigan. The cell-phone provider was Arch Wireless Holdings. The interesting discovery was to whom the call went. It was to the same person that had turned over the rental property to the bank, Jack Harding. It was a five-second call—probably plenty of time to say, "We got 'im."

The Burton and Flint Police Departments already had their eyes on Jack Harding. Could he be a kidnapper? Sure. Jack was suspected of illegal gun sales and illegal gambling activities. They

175

were certain he was involved in loan sharking, but they hadn't been able to pin charges on him yet. According to the IRS, his books always seemed to stand up to their scrutiny. Hutch's opinion was that Jack Harding was capable of just about anything. Maybe they had finally caught a break and could nail him for kidnapping. The big question was why would he be involved in a kidnapping? Maybe Clay Thomas would have an idea.

Since it was Friday, Hutch decided he would head to Flint Southwestern Academy for the basketball game that evening. He'd been hearing that Tanner Thomas was one of the top players around, maybe even around the whole state. He could take in the game and then talk with Clay Thomas to see if there could possibly be any motive for Jack Harding to kidnap his son, Tanner.

***

Clay tried Jessie's cell phone one more time, and again, it went straight to her voicemail. Once he was sure that Tanner was gone, he drove toward home, hoping that Jessie would be there. When he saw her car in the garage, he had second thoughts, and he started to wonder what to do. He finally decided to head into the house, and he prayed for wisdom. What could he possibly say to her to make things right?

Chapter 29

When Clay entered the house, Jessie looked up at him, surprised. She had been crying. Clay felt sorrow that he should cause her any grief. He wanted desperately to make things right.

"Hi, Honey," he said softly. "Are you all right?"

Immediately, Jessie began crying again. Clay wanted to go to her, but he held back and waited. Jessie's green eyes were always so expressive, and what they suggested as Clay gently looked at her was guilt.

"Clay...you said that you only manipulated my mind one time?"

"Just in the hospital that one time. That's the truth, Jessie. I wish you would forgive me."

"Why did you do it?"

Clay took a deep breath. "You were so distraught about what might happen to Tanner and about not being able to get pregnant again. I hated seeing you that way. You said it was your fault. You were blaming yourself, and I didn't want you to feel that guilt the rest of your life."

Jessie hesitated before saying, "Clay, I need you to forgive me too."

"No, you don't. I forgave you as soon as I heard Tanner was born and you were both doing well. I loved you then as much as I do now."

"This is something different, Clay. I did something wrong."

Clay was confused. He had told her to forget in the hospital. She couldn't be remembering, could she? Clay had wondered occasionally if she would ever recall anything from that day, but she never brought it up, even though at times he sensed she felt some sort of lingering guilt. *Clay* certainly never intended to talk about it. He had told her that it wasn't her fault and that she shouldn't blame herself. Why was she bringing it up now after all these years? "I don't understand," Clay said.

Jessie took a deep breath and tried to control the tears that were streaming down her cheeks. Clay gave her time to compose herself. Finally Jessie said, "I was with another man."

"I know."

"How could you know?"

"Because I saw you."

Jessie was shocked. "You followed me?" Jessie had seen no indication that Clay was suspicious of her relationship with John. He never seemed to notice *anything*. Why would he have been following her?

"No, I just happened to be driving by when I saw you get out of his car. He helped you to your car and then just drove away."

Now Jessie was confused. "What are you talking about? When did you see that?"

"I was driving by—it was just pure coincidence—and I saw you get out of a man's car. Then I saw him get out and help you to your own car. I pulled into a parking lot and watched him drive away. Then I followed you to the hospital."

"To the hospital? I never went to the hospital!"

"Of course you went to the hospital." How could she remember and not know that? "It was where Tanner was born. But you got there in time, Jessie. The doctors saved Tanner, and he's all right. Not having more children wasn't the end of the world. I forgave you because I loved you. I told you to forget. I used my mind powers and told you to forget, and that it wasn't your fault. I didn't want you living with the guilt your whole life. I thought that I took care of it. I'm sorry, Jessie."

"Clay, I was with him yesterday. I never went to the hospital."

178

Now it was Clay's turn to be confused. They didn't seem to be talking about the same thing. "I'm talking about the day Tanner was born, Jessie. You were with another man that day. I used to think about it a lot. You must have been with him when your water broke. You knew Tanner was breech, and you must have known something was wrong right away. But you didn't rush to the hospital like you should have. You couldn't do that because you were with him in *his* car. So instead of going to the hospital, he drove you back to your car, and then you had to drive to emergency from there. Who knows how long the delay was, but there was certainly a delay."

Jessie was sitting with her mouth hanging open. She didn't remember any of that happening. She was intending to tell Clay about John. She needed Clay to forgive her for what she had done yesterday afternoon. Clay had hidden things from her their whole marriage, but he claimed that he had always loved her and never manipulated her, except one time in the hospital. After she slept with John, though, and got a taste of his temper, she realized it was Clay who really loved her. She had wanted to confess to Clay, but what she was hearing now was incredible.

"I followed you to the hospital and turned into a lot to park the car. I guess you collapsed while I was parking and paramedics rushed you inside. When I finally got to the check in window, I heard someone say that they needed to call me. When they realized that I was there already, they sent me to labor and delivery. During that whole delay, they already had wheeled you into the operating room."

Something was stirring in the back of Jessie's mind. She had often somehow felt guilt in her life, but she had never understood the feeling. Was this why she felt that lingering guilt for so long?

"You're telling me that I was with another man on the day that Tanner was born? I was having an affair?"

"I needed to know, so I did a little investigating, and yes, I found that you were having an affair while you were pregnant with Tanner."

"And you told me to forget?"

"I told you to forget—that the delivery problems weren't your fault."

"So for all these years, you've known my guilt, and you've hidden it from me? I'm responsible for almost killing my son and for ruining our chance to have more children?"

"You can't know that for sure. And I don't care about the affair. I loved you enough to forgive you." Jessie looked devastated, so Clay pleaded with her. "I've been hiding my secret and yours our whole marriage, Jessie, but it's out now. I need you to forgive me for keeping *both* secrets. Please, Jessie, please."

"I didn't know you, and I didn't even know myself all these years," Jessie nearly whispered. She looked to be in shock. Tears began flowing down her cheeks again. Clay stepped forward to embrace her, but she backed away. "You knew these things, and you forgave me?" She seemed lost in a flood of questions, emotions, and newly found guilt, yet she didn't know what to do or say, so she grabbed her things that she had already gathered for Tanner's game, and she left the house and drove away.

Clay was left wondering what it was that Jessie had been talking about. Who was she with yesterday? Why did she need him to forgive her? What had she done wrong? Clay obviously had been suspicious of Jessie recently. Was she planning on telling him about John when he mixed everything up? Clay had told her the whole story before he figured out that she hadn't remembered *anything* about the earlier affair; she had been intending to tell him about her most recent one. Now with Jessie gone, he could only hope that she would end up at Tanner's game and he would get another chance to make things right. Whatever she had done, he knew he could forgive her again. He was more worried about whether she would ever forgive him.

Chapter 30

The game was the last scheduled basketball game before a long Christmas break. As part of their attempt to strengthen their schedule, the Kearsley Hornets were playing the Knights of Flint Southwestern Academy on the Knight's home court. The Knights featured the Jones twins, two of the most heralded juniors in the state. Their names, Earvin and Gervin, were in honor of two of the NBA's greatest players, Earvin "Magic" Johnson and George Gervin. Many believed that the brothers could be destined to follow their namesakes to the NBA. Both were high intensity players who talked a lot of smack and who weren't above a hard foul or two, leading to an occasional technical foul call. Two things were certain, however. They played very well together, and they were extremely talented.

When Goodrich High School's team played at Flint Southwestern just two weeks prior to the Kearsley contest, the car windows of three different cars had been smashed in the parking lot. In addition, in a non-league game a week and a half later against Saginaw Buena Vista, there were unconfirmed rumors of two separate fights. Because of the stories, there wasn't as good of a crowd turnout for the visitors as usual, and the Hornet fans were outnumbered more than two to one. It was going to be an unusually difficult playing environment, and many college scouts, news writers, and bloggers were wondering how Tanner Thomas would respond.

Jessie and Clay arrived separately and sat separately, though they were able to keep an eye on each other, and Clay was keeping a close eye on his wife. Detective Hutchinson and Officer Janski were in attendance, and the city of Flint had a contingent of officers on hand at the game, as well. Jack Harding was seated alone in a far top corner of the visitor's bleachers. Dr. Zander Frauss and an assistant coach for the University of Michigan basketball team snuck in just before tip-off and took a seat behind the Southwestern Academy team bench. Mark Simpson, looking a little sluggish, and his wife, Carlee, were also late arrivals to the game.

The game started with both the Jones brothers guarding Tanner. The other three defenders were playing a 2-1 zone. The two Knight defenders at the top of the zone were shading Luke and Kevin closely, while the one player defending down low in the zone was paying close attention to Sprout Monroe. This odd defense generally left Mike Powell, the weakest offensive player, open. The Jones brothers were both trash talking from the opening tip. Defensively for the Hornets, they were playing a 3-2 zone because neither Luke nor Kevin was quick enough to cover either of the Jones brothers man-to-man. It was a raucous crowd, the Knight's coach was intimidating, and the Southwestern players were quick and extremely aggressive.

The game started with a double team on Tanner, a hack across his wrists, no foul call, a turnover, and an easy basket for Gervin Jones. On the second possession against full-court pressure, Kevin Harding was swarmed, knocked to the floor, and another turnover resulted when no foul call was made. It was Earvin who converted the second basket. Coach Piggott was already screaming his head off and the game was only 30 seconds old. The pressure continued and each time the referees called a foul on Southwestern, the crowd went nuts, and the coach had a fit. It seemed like each time there was no foul call, often with a resulting turnover, Coach Piggott would blow a gasket. Intensity was high, and the Kearsley players were getting nearly assaulted. At the end of the first quarter, Flint Southwestern had an 18-6 lead, but they had already

182

committed eight fouls and Kearsley was in the bonus and shooting free throws. Earvin and Gervin Jones both had two fouls, and Tanner had already made four free throws. The only basket came on an assist from Tanner to Mike Powell, who was left unguarded under the basket.

As the teams took the floor to begin the second quarter, a shoving match ensued between Luke Simms and a Knight player. Both were assessed technical fouls, but the foul was the Knight player's third and the team's ninth, so the Hornets would be shooting the double bonus for the remainder of the half. The player, one of the Knight's quickest athletes, was forced to sit on the bench. Southwestern's coach screamed at the referees, screamed at his player, and screamed at Coach Piggott. The intensity picked up another notch. On a drive to the basket, Tanner was violently knocked to the floor by Earvin Jones, who stood over Tanner and said, "Don't you be bringin' that weak 'mess' to *my* house!" (Except he didn't say "mess"). Before the referee could "T" him up, Mike Powell gave Jones a shove, resulting in his own technical foul, but somehow in the melee that ensued, and after order was restored, Earvin Jones's poor sportsmanship was overlooked, saving him from his fourth foul. Tanner made his two free throws, but Gervin Jones shot the two technical free throws at the other end, and he also made them both. When the Knights were given the ball out of bounds, Kearsley's fans were screaming about the oversight, and Southwestern's fans responded with even more vigor. Midway through the period, when a Knight player was called for an over-the-back foul on an offensive rebound, the Southwestern coach laid into the referees once again. He called a time out to chew out his players as well. Several of the police officers were talking nervously on the sidelines. It was beginning to look like things could get out of hand.

On the way to the bench, Tanner Thomas did a strange thing. He walked over to Southwestern's head coach, coolly looked him in the eyes, and said very calmly and clearly, "Listen to me, Coach. You're showing very bad sportsmanship. We have two good teams here, but the game's getting outta control. You need to be a better example to your players and your fans. You need to be a leader and calm down." Then he smiled a big smile, shook the coach's hand, and walked to his bench for the remainder of the time out. There he told Coach Piggott to calm down as well. Both coaches smiled, talked calmly to their players, and sent them back onto the court.

Sprout made the first of two free throws coming out of the time-out, but when he missed the second, there was a tremendous fight for the ball, ending in a loose ball and a pile-up on the court. The pile-up was turning ugly when all of a sudden, Tanner, whose intensity had peaked to a new level, yelled, "Everyone, *STOP!*" And *everyone* stopped. "This craziness has to stop!" Even the crowd was quiet. "We have two good teams. We should be playing a good game. Let's just play basketball!"

Southwestern's coach walked to the floor, put his arm around Tanner Thomas, and spoke up very clearly. "This young man is right. This isn't what high school sports is all about. It's a *game*. We have a responsibility to show sportsmanship or we shouldn't be playing. I apologize for my behavior. And I commend Tanner Thomas for speaking out." He began to clap, and the fans in the stands followed suit.

The coach shook Tanner's hand again, and returned to his bench. Clay turned to look at his wife, who had a dumbfounded look on her face. She looked at her husband, who mouthed the words, "His mind-powers are *very* strong."

When the referees went to the scorer's table to sort out the previous play, Earvin and Gervin Jones spoke to Tanner. "Let's play some ball," Earvin said with a smile.

"Let's see what kind of player you really are," Gervin said as he offered his hand to Tanner.

"Okay…let's do it," Tanner responded.

***

With the Jones twins both in foul trouble, they settled back into a traditional man-to-man defense, and the real game began. At half-time the score was 34-22. Tanner had made one basket and nine of ten free throws. In the second half, however, he exploded. Both teams played with a poise and intensity rarely seen in a high

184

school game. The Knight's coach encouraged and praised and patted his players on the back. Pete Piggott sat calmly on the bench. Fans cheered instead of complaining, and what a great game they were to witness. At the end of the third period, the score was 56-50. Fifty points were scored in the third period, but it was nothing compared to the fourth. Tanner lit it up for 18 third quarter points, while the Jones brothers were making one remarkable shot after another. Tanner had 29 points, while both Joneses had twenty-two.

There was rarely a possession in the fourth quarter that didn't end in a score. Earvin Jones committed his fourth foul with seven minutes remaining in the game and sat on the bench for four minutes. In those four minutes, Tanner led his team to a two-point advantage. With three minutes to go, Earvin reentered the game and scored on a three-point play the first time he touched the ball, giving his team the lead back by one point. From there, each team scored on every possession, and heading into the last two possessions, the lead had changed hands 12 consecutive times.

With 11 seconds remaining and Kearsley down by one point, they took the ball out of bounds on their own offensive sideline. No one guarded Luke Simms as he took the ball out of bounds, and once again, both of the twins covered Tanner. Tanner was posted on the ball-side block on the right side, underneath his own basket. Kevin and Mike lined up on the wing opposite the ball. Sprout flashed to the ball and received a lob pass from Luke. When he stepped inbounds, Sprout immediately returned the pass to Luke, who drove baseline to his right, right in the direction of the spot that Tanner had vacated. Tanner cut across the lane in the opposite direction and received a screen first from Mike, then from Kevin, and then from Sprout, as he circled all the way around the court and back toward the side of Luke's drive. A Knight defender was forced to stop Luke Simms. Luke pulled up about six feet from the basket and rose for a jump shot, but instead of shooting, he fired a hard right-handed pass to Tanner Thomas on the run. Quarterback passing to wide-receiver, just like in the football season. Tanner received the pass in stride and lofted an 18 foot jump shot that hit nothing but the bottom of the net. Kearsley had taken the lead again by one point. The Knights called their last time-out.

There were 3.8 seconds remaining and Flint Southwestern Academy had to go the length of the court to score. The only information Coach Piggott gave in the huddle was to play man-to-man and not to foul. Southwestern was in the penalty and would shoot free throws after any foul. There was almost complete silence in the gym as the Knights took the ball out of bounds. The inbounds passer hurled a long, three-quarter-court pass down the court. Earvin Jones leapt high in the air, and without landing, passed the ball to his brother who was sprinting down the court past his twin. Gervin caught the pass from his brother, took two dribbles ahead, planted, and let fly a three-pointer from the far right corner with Tanner Thomas's hand in his face. The shot hung in the air for what seemed like eternity, the silence in the crowd giving the moment an eerie, surreal feeling. The ball appeared to rotate in slow motion while everything else seemed motionless and silent. The clock wound down in super-slow speed as the ball continued to float toward the basket, banging off the back of the rim, and ricocheting down through the net. The Knights had won the game, 84-82. Sixty points had been scored in the fourth quarter and the lead had changed in each of the last 14 possessions. Gervin Jones had scored 34, Earvin Jones 30, and Tanner Thomas, a game and career-high, 47. He had scored 36 points in the second half alone.

After the game, the twins went to Tanner. "You're one sweet ballplayer, I gotta tell ya," Gervin said.

"Best I ever played against," Earvin added, "includin' my stupid brother here." He was smiling like crazy. "You *know* I shoulda got that last shot, 'stead of you."

"Coach had *me* shootin' 'cause he knew youda never made it."

"Shoot, man. He knew you couldn'ta jumped high enough to catch that pass. Had ta have me *catchin'* that pass or we woulda never even got no shot off."

"Great game, you guys," Tanner said with a smile. "You played an awesome game." They shook hands and walked off the court with the respect that only truly great players can have for each other.

As Tanner headed for the locker room, he heard Southwestern's coach tell a newspaper reporter that Tanner Thomas should be given credit for the greatest game he'd ever been a part of. "It was Tanner Thomas," he said, "who convinced two teams, two coaches, and a crowd of angry people that high school athletics is about sportsmanship and self-control. Not only is Tanner Thomas a great basketball player, but a great leader who should be commended."

Tanner smiled as he continued to the locker room because there was one thing he knew that no one else except possibly his mother and father knew: he had used his powers to influence, in a positive way, a whole gymnasium full of people. Tanner had used his powers not for a selfish reason, but to accomplish something good.

Jeff La Ferney

Chapter 31

When the game ended, Jack Harding exited quickly and headed for his office. Zander and the University of Michigan coach had both seen exactly what they had hoped to see when they showed up for the game. Dr. Frauss was seated right behind the Southwestern coach when Tanner spoke to him in the second quarter, and then he had witnessed Tanner change the personality of an entire gym full of people. He was certain that Tanner had used his mind-control. The Michigan coach had witnessed an exhibition of maturity, leadership, and talent rarely displayed by a high school player. He was certain that Tanner could be a leader in Michigan's basketball program. Satisfied, they also immediately left the gym. The Flint City police officers were extremely pleased to watch a gymnasium full of fans from opposing schools peacefully emptying the stands to comments such as, "That was the best basketball game I've ever seen." Smiles were exhibited and high fives and handshakes were shared.

Clay looked over at Jessie, who was crying once again, partly out of pride for her son and partly out of shame. Clay walked over to her and asked her if she was okay. "Yes. I think I'm going to be fine, eventually. There's a lot of information and a lot of emotions swirling in my head right now, but I want you to come back home tonight, and maybe this time, the *three* of us can talk."

"How about I give Tanner a set of my car keys? We can drop my car off at the school for Tanner and then go home together."

"I have something I have to do first. You pick Tanner up at the school and go back home. I'll be there soon, and we can all talk." She wiped her eyes with a tissue and headed out of the gym.

***

Detectives Hutchinson and Janski found Clay and walked up to him. Hutch extended his hand and said, "Congratulations on a great game, Mr. Thomas. Can't say if I've ever seen a better one, and can't say if I've ever seen a better performance. He's quite a player, and quite a mature young man, too."

"That's for sure," Janski agreed. "What a game!"

"Thank you. I'm speechless, to be honest. I don't know what to say. Thank you."

Several other parents and fans patted Clay Thomas on the back and shook hands as if Clay had something to do with Tanner's performance or deserved some sort of honor. It was Tanner's night, but Clay certainly felt a great deal of pride.

"I believe I arrested that loud-mouthed coach of his 'bout 15 years ago for drunk and disorderly," Hutch commented. "He hasn't changed much, 'cept he's fatter…. I don't mean to interrupt the moment, Mr. Thomas," he apologized, "but we need to talk. We have some information that I think you should know."

They moved away from the pockets of people that were still lingering on the gym floor. "We've investigated some of the leads we have, thanks to Tanner, and it's led us to the man we think is responsible for the kidnapping. We followed the paper trail for the house ownership, and we've discovered who received the phone call from the kidnapper. Both leads point to the same person."

"You have a name?"

"Yes, sir. We believe the man behind the kidnapping of your son is a Mr. Jonathon 'Jack' Harding."

Clay's heart skipped a couple of beats and his knees almost buckled. "How can that be? Why? Why would he ever want to kidnap Tanner?"

"That's what we want to know. Think about it, Clay. The kidnapper said it was for revenge more than 20 years overdue. It must not've been about Tanner. Is it about you?"

190

"I just don't see how. I know he was pressuring Tanner's coach to play his son more at the point, but I don't see what else he could possibly have against me. I didn't even *know* the man until his son and daughter moved into the school district less than two years ago. It doesn't make sense."

"Well, we figured he'd be at the game tonight. Now that it's over, we'll be heading over to his house with a warrant for his arrest. We wanted you to know…and we hoped you'd help with a motive. I guess we'll have to figure that out next. Hey, Clay, we're gonna nail this guy. He's a career crook—one of the bad guys. There's a lotta people gonna be happy to have him put away." He shook hands again with Clay. "Your son played great. Tell him I said so." Then he and his partner headed away on official police business.

***

As Clay watched him walk away, Carlee grabbed his arm. "Where's Jessie?" she asked.

"Hi, Carlee. She's already gone. Said she had something she had to do before coming home." He saw the look of concern on her face. "Is something wrong?"

She hesitated as if trying to make up her mind, but finally, she replied. "I'm worried about her, Clay. Maybe I'll lose her friendship by breaking her trust, but I've found out something about her that I think you need to know." She hesitated again.

"What is it? You need to tell me."

"Jessie told me that she's been seeing someone. I tried to discourage her, but she wouldn't listen. She told me some things that made me worry, so I had her followed. I have some pictures, Clay, taken yesterday afternoon. I was told this is a bad, bad guy she's been seeing, and I'm worried."

Clay impatiently pulled the envelope and pictures from her hand. He flipped through them in embarrassment. The first was of the Super 8 Motel, that cheap motel on Dort Highway; then of his wife talking on a black phone in her car—the prepaid phone he had discovered in her purse. The next picture was of her entering room number 12. The next picture, he discovered with a look of horror.

It was just outside room twelve and it was of Jack Harding. Jonathon Jack Harding. In his head, he once again plainly heard the word, "John." His wife was having an affair with the man who had kidnapped Tanner! He barely noticed the next picture of his wife exiting the motel room. He simply said, "Jessie's in trouble."

Chapter 32

Jessie got in her car and pulled out her prepaid TracFone, assuming it would be the last time she would need to use it. There was notification of a message, so she went to her voicemail. It was John—Jack Harding. He was apologizing and asking her to come to his office after the game. She was intending to call him to ask to meet, so she simply put her phone away and headed for Harding Metals. It was time for her to end the relationship.

Jessie parked her car in the small lot outside the scrap yard. One gate was unlocked, so she walked through and entered the office building. Jack was sitting in his office behind his desk, but he jumped up with a smile when he saw Jessie. He went to her and put his arms around her. "Thanks so much for coming. You got my message, so you know I want to apologize. I'm sorry for getting upset yesterday. Please, forgive me."

Jessie pulled away. "I forgive you, John, but I have another reason for coming. I've made a mistake. Things went too fast and too far. I have to break it off. I just have to. I'm sorry."

"No, Jessie. You *can't* break it off. I love you. You love me too."

"No, I don't. I love Clay. I misunderstood some things and overreacted. Clay loves me too."

The anger was flashing in Jack Harding's eyes once again. "He doesn't love you; he only loves himself. He's been manipulating you his whole life. You couldn't possibly love Clay Thomas. You love me."

193

"No, I don't."

"You'll love me if I tell you to love me!" he nearly screamed.

"You can't make me love you!" Jessie shot back.

"Oh, yes I can." He walked to his desk and returned with a stack of pictures and a videotape. He handed the pictures to her. "I said I had somethin' special for you. Take a look at those."

To her amazement, Jessie began looking at a series of photos of her and Harding at each of their various rendezvous. They were walking in Dow Gardens, hand in hand. They were eating lunch together. She was receiving flowers, a purse, jewelry. They were kissing. She was entering a motel room. It was creepy and disgusting. "You've had someone following us? This whole relationship has been staged? And you say that you love me? You disgust me!"

He was actually smiling. "And this." He held up the videocassette. "This is evidence of our time together yesterday."

"You're sick! We were *videotaped*? What are you doing? What do you want?"

"Either you love me like I want or I show them to your mind-controlling husband. Either decision you make is fine with me. Both options hurt your husband and nothing gives me greater pleasure than hurting your husband. Either I take something from him that he supposedly cares about," he sarcastically said, "or I get to show him that his wife is a cheater—that she cheated on him with *me*."

"I don't have any idea what you have against Clay, but I know one thing for sure. I will *never* love you." Jessie, with all the pictures and the video in hand, turned to head for the door.

She heard a click, and Jack Harding forcefully said, "Stop right there, or I'll shoot you dead."

Jessie turned and saw that he was aiming a gun directly at her. "What are you going to do, kidnap me?"

"Why not? I had Tanner kidnapped. Why not you?"

"You did *what*? You're a sickening, disgusting man."

"You didn't think so yesterday. You have the video to prove it. Now bring those back to me and sit down. Hurting Clay gives

194

me pleasure to no end, but with you here, maybe there's still some pleasure I can get from you."

Terrified, Jessie sat as far from Jack as she could get. She didn't know what it was, ESP? Clairvoyance? Regardless of what it was, she began focusing on Clay and Tanner with all her might. Maybe if she could focus hard enough, someone would come for her.

***

As soon as Tanner stepped out of the locker room, Clay rushed to him. Keeping out of earshot of the other players, Clay said, "Your mother's in trouble. The kidnapper was Jack Harding, and I think she went to see him. Tell me, Tanner, is there any way that you can find her? You found the house; maybe you can find your mother."

Clay turned and found Coach Piggott. "Coach, I need Tanner to ride with me. It's a family emergency. Jessie's missing."

"If it's got anything at all to do with Jack Harding, then you got my blessing to do whatever you need to do."

"What do you know about Jack, Pete?"

"I know I work for him, and he's a piece o' horse crap, if ya don't mind my sayin' so, and I'm sorry, Clay, but my cousin, Carlee Simpson, had me followin' yer wife, and I saw 'em together yesterday."

"You're the one who followed her? Things are getting crazier and crazier. We have to go, Pete. Thanks."

"And I think I love her," Pete Piggott thought to himself. *"First I can't have Honey Suckle, and now I can't have Jessie Thomas. At least I have good taste in women."*
***

Clay and Tanner ran to Clay's car as fast as they could. Once in the car, Clay called Hutch. He figured the detective would probably be closing in on the Harding house, and he would be only a few minutes behind Jessie if that was where she was headed. When he arrived, he could let Clay know if Jessie was there. He asked Hutch to call him as soon as he knew anything. He then called Jessie's cell phone, but it rang several times and then went

195

to voicemail. Jessie had left her purse in the car as usual. She wouldn't even know that he was trying to reach her. Clay pondered where she would go if she was going to see Harding. He wondered if maybe they would go back to that sleazy motel. He drove like a man possessed down I-69 and then turned off on Dort Highway. He zoomed down the road heading south at about 65 miles per hour. In just a few minutes, he spotted the building, but when he turned into it, Jessie's car wasn't there. He hoped Tanner wouldn't ask questions. He hesitated. Again he strained to think of where she could be.

"At the scrap yard!" they both said at the same time. And just then, Clay had a sensation in his head that someone was talking to him. "Did you hear that?" he asked Tanner.

"I didn't hear anything." Tanner was looking all around outside for the source of some sound that his father heard.

"It was in my head. It's like your mother is calling for help. And I don't know how I know this, but I'm certain she's at Harding Metals. Hang on!" Clay raced back onto Dort Highway, heading north this time at an even faster clip.

About two minutes later, Detective Hutchinson called. "She's not here, Clay. I don't think anyone's here. We have a warrant, so I'm gonna look around a bit."

"Hutch, I think she's at Harding Metals. I think she's with Jack. I need you to get over there as soon as you can."

"Clay, I've got to check this place out first and make sure he's not here. It should only take a minute and then we'll head right over there, lights flashing."

Just then, it started to rain. It was an icy December rain. Clay's wipers still didn't work well, and the roads immediately started to get slippery. He was forced to slow down, but his blood pressure was speeding up. Both Clay and Tanner said at the same time, "I hate rain."

Chapter 33

After the longest ten minutes of his life, Clay pulled into the small front lot of Harding Metals. Jessie's car was sitting in the lot, windows accumulating the sleety rain. He parked and hesitated. What if he caught his wife doing something he didn't want to see? But then the voice in his head returned. *"Help me, Clay! Help me, Tanner!"* it said.

"What are we waiting for?" Tanner asked impatiently.

"To be honest, I wasn't sure what to do, but I'm hearing the voice again. Your mother's in trouble. We have to go."

Clay and Tanner climbed out of the car and, shielding their faces from the rain, jogged through the open gate. Clay pulled open the office doors and they stepped inside.

"No! Get your hands off me!" they heard Jessie cry.

When they reached the office they could see that Jack was holding Jessie from behind, a hand on each breast. He appeared to be kissing her neck as Jessie was trying to fight out of his grasp.

"Get your hands off her!" Clay yelled.

Immediately, Jack released her and she ran to her husband.

"Well, well, well, if it isn't Clay the psychic. What am I thinking, Clay?" Jack asked sarcastically. He pulled out his gun once again and aimed it at Clay.

"What're you doing, Jack? What's going on here, and why would you kidnap Tanner?'

"You came for answers. Of course—something selfish. And here I thought you were here to rescue your slutty wife."

Clay's eyes were on the gun. "Put the gun down, Jack. There's no need for violence."

"I'll tell you what, Clay. I'll answer your questions, and then I'll shoot you. I'm doing all of this for revenge."

"Revenge? I don't get it. I've only known you for a couple of years. What did I do?"

"A couple years? Think again, Thomas. All the way back to high school."

"You didn't go to high school with me."

"No, but I went to Okemos. Played football and basketball."

Clay gave no indication of remembering him.

"For football," Jack continued, "I was the kicker. Twice you humiliated me in the game our senior year. Remember how I missed the game winning field goal?" He was trying to jar Clay's memory.

Some recollection finally came to Clay. "You got in my face and told me we were gonna lose. That was you?"

"Yep. You told me I was gonna miss, and I did. You ran the kick in for a touchdown and knocked me on my butt along the way. It was humiliating. My teammates and classmates never let me live that down. And now I find out you can control minds. You got into my head, didn't you, Clay?"

"I wouldn't have done a thing if you weren't such a cocky butthead. You came to me, remember? But yes, I prob'ly got in your head."

"And if that wasn't bad enough, you did it again in basketball."

Again, Clay was drawing a blank.

"You made me miss the game winning free throws at the end."

The memory dawned on Clay once again. "You're the punk who pushed me into the wall?"

"Yeah, just trying to even things up."

"And then later you shoved me and got T'd up."

"But I had a chance to win the game anyway, until you got in my head."

"What I remember is you getting in my grill again, telling me we were gonna lose. So I told you that you'd miss."

"Well, I missed all right, and then you gave me this." He pointed to his crooked nose. "You broke my nose, Thomas." Again, Clay showed no signs of recollection. "I was the class laughing stock the rest of the year. You broke my nose. I lost my starting position. And it's your fault! I hated you with a passion, and then how does fate treat me? We end up in the same city where your son takes all the attention from mine *and* is dating my daughter! So I decided to take some things from you.

"First, I tried to keep your son out of Kevin's way on the basketball court," Jack continued. "Nothin' seemed to work. I assume you and Tanner here had something to do with that. Used your mind powers somehow. So I figured I'd put you through a little hell by nabbing Tanner; maybe make a few ransom dollars in the process. Guess Tanner here made sure that didn't work out. Figured if I took your wife away, that'd make me pretty happy too. She's not bad in the sack either, Clay. Wanta see some pictures?"

"You're a disgusting human being! And you're miserable aren't you? Revenge? From high school? You should just let it go, Jack. And you should just let us go."

***

Pete Piggott rode the bus back to the school then grabbed a quick bite to eat from a drive-through on the way to work. He was getting there a little early. The sleeting rain put him in a bad mood. When he pulled into the parking lot at Harding Metals, he had a bad, bad feeling. There in the lot was Jessie Thomas's car, along with Jack's and one other. Either they'd moved from motel to office and were doing it again, or Jessie was in trouble. If Pete was a betting man, he'd put money on Jessie Thomas being in trouble, and he wasn't going to let any woman he loved be hurt by Jack Harding. He reached into his coat pocket, touching the now familiar .22. He fought his way out of the car, the steering wheel, as always, interfering with his fat frame. He saw that he didn't need his key for the gate; it was already open. He opened the door and heard talking as he crept his way toward Jack's office.

199

"Don't be playing any mind games on me, Clay. You either, Tanner. Step away from the door, and move over to this wall." Jack pointed to the wall opposite the door. The sleety rain was coming down harder now, showering the metal roof above, the tapping sounds almost certainly drowning out Pete Piggott's heavy breathing. Jack had his gun pointed at Clay Thomas, his back to the office door.

Clay pulled Jessie behind him. "The police know you kidnapped Tanner. I called them before I came here. They'll be here soon. Whatever you're thinking, you won't get away with it."

"You're prob'ly just tryin' to get in my head, Thomas, but do you think I really care? I've been lookin' forward to hurtin' you for a long, long time."

Jessie stepped out from behind Clay. "You'll be in jail. What about Kevin and TJ?"

"They got their mother. They'll be all right. Things've gone too far to stop now. It's time to finish what I started." He raised his gun, pointing it directly at Clay.

Clay immediately thought, *"Don't shoot me."*

At the same time, Tanner was thinking, *"Don't shoot him."*

Jack lowered his gun. "I just got the distinct message in my head that I shouldn't shoot you, Clay. Did you or Tanner send me that message? Okay, I won't shoot you." Immediately he aimed his gun a little to the left and fired a bullet directly into the chest of Jessie.

Clay grabbed her as she fell, and then he heard, *"NO!!!"*

He looked up as Pete Piggott barreled through the doorway, gun in hand. The gun was firing shot after shot, ten shots in all. Jack whirled and fired back, and by the time Pete Piggott's magazine was completely empty, Jack had managed to fire a couple of slugs into the rampaging man. When Pete fell, it was directly onto the body of the dead Jack Harding.

Chapter 34

"Jessie!" Clay lowered her to the floor. The bullet had entered the middle of her chest and had actually exited her back and struck the wall behind. She was bleeding terribly. Clay pulled a handkerchief from his pocket and pressed it to the chest wound. He held a hand over the wound on her back, but blood was still spreading quickly across the floor. She was already breathing shallowly. "Call 9-1-1!" Clay shouted to Tanner.

Tanner punched in the numbers. When the operator answered, he shouted, "There's been a shooting! Harding Metals! We need an ambulance!" He snapped his phone shut and kneeled in the blood beside his father.

"Hang on, Jessie. Please hang on," Clay pleaded. "Don't die on me. Please hang on."

Jessie, whose eyes had been closed, managed to get them to flutter open. "I'm so sorry, Clay. I'm so sorry I hurt you again."

"It's okay. I forgive you. It doesn't matter. Just hang on. I don't want to lose you."

"Please, Mom, don't die," Tanner begged.

"I love you, Clay. I really do," she whispered. "I love you, Tanner." She was fading fast.

"I never made you love me. You know that, right?" Tears were dropping from Clay's eyes.

"I know that...think I always knew. So sorry to hurt you... Clay? Tanner? Do me a favor...please?" She was struggling to get the words out. She was dying.

"Anything, just don't die. Please," Clay begged.

"When it rains...remember me...don't hate the rain anymore."

Her eyes rolled back, and she died.

"No!" Clay cried. He laid her head back and began giving her mouth-to-mouth resuscitation. He breathed out some quick breaths and then pressed on her chest with his hands, bloodying them further. But Jessie was dead.

"Dad, she's gone," Tanner said, tears flowing down his cheeks. "She's gone."

***

Detective Hutchinson burst through the door, gun raised, assessing the violent scene before him. To the back of the office, Clay and Tanner were helplessly holding the body of their lifeless wife and mother. To his left, Jack Harding lay sprawled beneath the body of Tanner's fat basketball coach. Blood was pooling on the floor. He kicked away the gun that was still in Jack's hand, and felt for a pulse on Pete Piggott. "This one's alive! Get a team in here right now!"

Sirens were wailing as Detective Janski left the building to direct the paramedics. Other police cars were also arriving on the scene. The paramedics strained to load Pete Piggott onto a stretcher, but he was alive as they rushed him to the ambulance.

***

In the ensuing hour or so, Jessie and Jack's bodies were taken away, and Hutch gathered the final missing facts. "So Harding did all this to get revenge for some embarrassing high school moments? You don't hear too many stories more stupid than that."

"That and to hopefully get his son some extra recognition."

"I'm so sorry, Clay...Tanner. I wish this one could have had a happy ending. I truly am sorry." They shook hands and Hutch exited the building.

Emotionally, Clay was nearly drained, but before he suggested that he and Tanner also leave the crime scene, Clay put his arms around his son. He started crying again, and Tanner shed some additional tears as well. "It shouldn't have ended like this, Tanner.

She finally knew…we could have finally been completely happy together."

"Dad, I don't know exactly what you've gone through the last 30 years, but I have an idea. You've got me to talk to now, though."

Clay stepped back for a minute, and then actually smiled. "You couldn't have said a more perfect thing, Tanner. Thank you. Just maybe we'll get through this together." He placed a bloodstained hand on Tanner's head and ruffled his hair. "Let's get out of here." They walked out of Harding Metals with Clay's arm draped around Tanner's shoulders, together.

Jeff La Ferney

Epilogue

Five months later, Clay and Tanner were sitting on their porch during a nice spring rain, just as Jessie always enjoyed doing. Neither was speaking, but both men knew what the other was thinking about. Jessie Thomas. When it rained, just as she had asked them to promise, they thought of her—Jessie, with her contagious personality, fantastic beauty, and unpredictable, free spirit. Tanner still missed her; she always had so much love for him. Clay's heart still mourned. He and Tanner were moving on with their lives, but their hearts continued to ache. It had been a beautifully sunny May day, but as Clay and Tanner returned home from Tanner's baseball game, it had started raining. They had instinctively walked straight to the porch and settled into their seats without bothering to go inside. Clay was learning to love the rain. Tanner seemed relieved to release the burden of hating rain that he had felt since childhood.

Finally, Clay spoke. "It's nice to see everything green again."

"I like the smell."

"You pitched a great game today, Tanner." Tanner had pitched a complete game, two-hit shutout.

"Thanks."

"You didn't...you know?"

"No, not one time, but I *wanted* to get into Corey Taylor's head. It would have been fun to make him look stupid. He's such an idiot, but I resisted the urge. The game was legit."

They sat there in silence some more. A lot had happened since they had lost Jessie. There was the funeral and a sad Christmas without her, but life forged ahead. Tanner wasn't himself for the first few basketball games in January, but that was expected. He came around soon, and finished off a great year. His team lost a game in the conference in January, the loss snapping Tanner out of his funk. They finished the regular season at 18-2, winning the conference championship and then also winning a district championship as well. They lost in the regionals to Saginaw High, and finished the season 21-3. Tanner made All-Conference and All-State first team. He accepted a basketball scholarship to the University of Michigan. Sammy Moretti of Toledo was the only other coach for whom Tanner seemed interested in playing, but Tanner had grown up favoring the Maize and Blue, and he had eventually learned that his dad had probably done more to "foil" the armed robbery than Coach Moretti had.

Kevin and TJ's mother came to Flint to stay with her kids until the end of the school year. TJ would be leaving for Toronto once summer arrived, but Kevin had decided to stay in his father's home and remain in Flint. Tanner broke up with TJ shortly after his mother died, not because of any anger toward TJ, but rather because it was so awkward to be around her. Jack's entire estate went to his two kids, TJ's to be put in a trust fund until she was 18. Kevin had a good basketball season, all things considered, and earned third-team all-league. He would be going to Baker College in Flint, a school where he was to earn a business degree, for he had decided to keep Harding Metals and continue to run the business.

Pete Piggott had survived, his fat body having protected him from death. He was in intensive care for several days and then began his recovery remarkably without complaint. He had a chance to start life over without Jack Harding controlling him. Luke Simm's father had taken over the basketball team as interim coach, but once Pete was back on his feet, he was determined to continue his career on the hardwood. As Piggott's health improved, he actually allowed Luke's father to stay on as assistant coach for the remainder of the season. Kevin had managed to persuade Coach Piggott to sue the estate of Jack Harding to get the money back that Jack had exploited from him through his illegal loans. Pete won, then took the money and bought TJ's share of Harding Metals, and Pete and Kevin became business partners. Kevin always was the only player that Pete much liked, and besides Honey Suckle, Jessie Thomas, and his cousin, Carlee, there really wasn't anybody else he much cared about. Pete was going to handle the majority of the business dealings while Kevin went to school. He was down to a nearly svelte 195 pounds and feeling much better about himself. When Johnny Papalli approached Piggott about continuing the business agreement that he had had with Jack Harding, Pete told him he could go back to whatever hole he crawled out of. Harding Metals was going to be a legitimate business and criminal elements were not welcome.

Clay had accepted an offer to become head baseball coach at the University of Michigan for the 2010 season. When the school year ended, father and son would move to Ann Arbor and start life over on the college campus, another reason why Tanner had chosen Michigan. In April, the winter semester had ended at Mott. Clay was still teaching the spring term, and his baseball season was winding down. Among those things, Tanner's high school baseball games, and some recruiting for U of M, Clay was keeping busy enough that his mind wasn't always on how much he missed his wife.

***

The phone rang inside the house, snapping Clay out of his quiet contemplation. He hustled inside and answered it.

"Hello."

"Hello, Clay? It's Zander...Zander Frauss."

"You're the only Zander I know, Doc. Last name's really not necessary."

Zander laughed. "How're you doin'?"

"Fine, thanks."

"How's Tanner?"

"We're getting by. What's up?"

"Well, I got wind of the fact that you accepted the head baseball job here. Congratulations."

"Thank you. It's a great opportunity, especially since Tanner's gonna to be there too."

"It *is* a great opportunity. I'm happy for you."

There was a long pause. Finally, Clay spoke. "I've known you long enough now, Zander, to know you've got something more on your mind than just congratulations. As a matter of fact, if I'm reading your mind correctly, you've got a proposition for me."

"Okay, I should have known that I can't hide anything from you. Are you going to finally let me do some tests?"

"Doc, Tanner and I can control minds. Between us, there've been episodes of ESP, telepathy, and clairvoyance. What more proof do you need that we have those abilities? I don't want you testing us like guinea pigs in your lab. And you already know what's causing it." By then Clay was back sitting on the porch with Tanner, enjoying the rain.

"All right, all right already. It's not just testing for the sake of testing that I want. Listen to me, Clay. I'm a believer that things happen to us in this life for a reason. You and Tanner have experienced a lot this past year, the current result being that you both are going to end up on the campus of the University of Michigan. I don't believe that it's a coincidence that it's here at the University that we have the Division of Perceptual Studies. In this laboratory, I may be able to help you and your son focus and enhance your powers."

"I don't see why we would want that, Zander," Clay interrupted. "I lost my wife; Tanner lost his mother, and the powers played a role in that."

"All things work together for good," Zander quoted. "There may be a higher purpose for this, Clay. There's a reason for everything."

"That's true, but I...*we*...don't want to hurt anyone else."

"I'm not asking you to hurt anyone; I'm asking you to help. My Division of Perceptual Studies is a serious scientific laboratory, quite possibly the best in the nation. I'm asking you to consider studying with me—you and Tanner both. There are things we can learn together. With the talents that the two of you have, a lot of valuable information could be learned in the field of parapsychology. What if we could duplicate or enhance your abilities scientifically? Let's talk in my office. Bring Tanner in and we'll talk."

"I'll...*we'll* think about it, Doc, but the answer will probably always be the same."

"I understand. You know how to reach me. I'll be talking to you again soon."

"I know," Clay smiled. "Believe me, I know."

***

When Clay hung up the phone, he returned to Tanner.

"Sounds like your friendly neuroscientist wants our cooperation."

"Thinks we can provide him with all his answers...and maybe help ourselves in the process," Clay answered.

"I was wondering when he was going to call."

"Me too. He was considering talking about it the last time I saw him. I read his mind. He didn't say anything then, but I've been expecting his call ever since."

"Dad?"

"Yes?"

"You've lived most of your life keeping your abilities a secret, right?"

"That's true."

"Do you believe your secret harmed your relationship with Mom and me?"

"I'd say that without question it did."

"How?"

"If your mom was to love me, I wanted to be sure that it was her choice, not mine. I loved your mom with all my heart, yet from the time you were born, I was never fully convinced that she loved me back. I was trapped. If I manipulated her, I'd have no satisfaction at all. If I told her the truth, she'd jump to the

209

conclusion that I'd been manipulating her all along...*and* I was pretty sure the truth would hurt her."

"You were right about that, weren't you?"

"Unfortunately, yes. Until the week of her death, she never learned the truth about me—and to some extent, herself—during 19 years of marriage, and in the meantime I did everything in my power to let her make her own decisions. She felt I lacked confidence, that I failed to give her the attention she deserved, that I wasn't the family leader that I needed to be. And it drove her to find satisfaction somewhere else because she didn't have the faith in me that she needed to have, and she didn't know me. Those choices she made seemed right to her at the time, but the end result was her death."

"You're not responsible for her choices, Dad. And you were always a good dad to me."

"Maybe. I loved you, but I couldn't be honest with you either. With you, I couldn't tell the truth because I couldn't be sure you could keep the secret. I didn't use my powers on you because I wanted you to make your own choices, develop your own values. I wanted to be proud of you because you were making good choices on your own. Because of that, you learned all of your values from your mom, who loved you in a way she wasn't comfortable loving me. I wasn't able to be the dad that other men could be because I felt I had to let you develop on your own, at your own pace. Oh, I loved you with all my heart, but I was determined not to *make* you be a good person. You needed to choose that path on your own. As a result, we were not close like you and your mother, and it was a constant source of unhappiness for me."

"Do you think you can be happy now?"

"I'm still grieving the loss of my wife, but I finally have two people who know the truth. I can be the father I always wanted to be, and I think in Zander I have a true friend for the first time since maybe high school. I think things are gonna be all right."

"So you're...*we're* going to work with Dr. Frauss?"

"You can make up your own mind about that," Clay remarked with a smile. "Me? I think I'm going to just take it one day at a time. My new friend will just have to be patient."

Tanner nodded his head and smiled. He and his dad looked intently out at the steadily drizzling rain as drops were falling from the trees' green leaves. After a lengthy pause in the conversation, they both said in unison, "I love the rain."

Jeff La Ferney

**Look for Books Two and Three in the series
Skeleton Key & Bulletproof**

Jeff La Ferney

About the Author

Jeff LaFerney has been a long-time language arts teacher and coach. He and his wife, Jennifer, as well as both of their kids, Torey and Teryn, live in Michigan. Jeff loves sports and exercise as well as reading and writing (his blog is called "The Red Pen"). *Skeleton Key* and *Bulletproof* are mysteries which also include Clay and Tanner Thomas. Each novel stands alone and can be read in any order. *Jumper* is a science fiction adventure and is the first in his Time Traveler series.

Made in the USA
Charleston, SC
20 February 2015